are saying about *The Spook's Apprentice*

'I grew up with this series. The characters have had an influence
over the person I am today: Tom's courage, Alice's strength,
Grimalkin's determination and self-confidence . . . what better
role models could there be for a teenager? Waiting for the release
of the next book every year, to spend some more time with these
characters who felt so real, was a torture, but finally holding each
new book in my hands made me feel so good.'

Marine Bornand

'I love the Spook's series for two main reasons.
The first is the atmosphere. Every detail counts and brings
something to the story. It's never too long or too much. The
second thing is the intensity of the story. There are situations
where there is no hope and suddenly a powerful help comes.
How the characters evolve throughout the books, how the plot
evolves with gravity. And what amazes me is that even if I know
the story, I read them with the same curiosity and rapidity.'

Nathalie Voirol

'I started reading Joseph Delaney's books when I was around thirteen. I noticed *The Spook's Apprentice* in the library and after reading it, I immediately wanted to continue reading the books. However, only the first three were translated into Hungarian. Since I wanted to continue reading them, I studied English passionately at school. At seventeen I was able to continue reading the books in English. Now I'm majoring in English and I can thank my love for literature to Joseph Delaney.'

Laura Zórity

'I love *The Spooks Apprentice* because it didn't shy away from the gory bits, and all of the witches were left-handed like me. It made me feel empowered.'

Aimee Collier

'I am not the greatest at reading and always struggled at school. But I grew up at the base of Pendle Hill and *The Spooks Apprentice* brought all the stories I grew up listening to, and the area I grew up in, into one cohesive series. I love it and always looked forward to the next book in the Wardstone universe.'

Ben Gowans

'*The Spook's Apprentice* has a special place in my heart. It was the first book I fell in love with, and I then read with enthusiasm all the books written by Joseph Delaney. He soon became my favourite writer, and Tom Ward will always be my favourite character. My biggest dream is to meet Joseph Delaney. I want to thank him for this wonderful series, which, luckily, isn't over yet.'

Emilia Oana

'I was in Year 8 when I first read *The Spook's Apprentice*. The greatest thing about the book and the books that followed is Joseph's ability to write in a way that makes each occurrence feel like a possibility. I even invited Joseph to my secondary school in inner-city Nottingham to talk to other students about the book – and he came with his wife, who was lovely in her pointy shoes! I've still got my signed copy of the American version that he gave me. Those books meant a lot to me.'

Hari Parekh

'Nothing else is quite like the Spook's series, and I have never found any other books I have liked so much. I can read them over and over again and always look out for any new books Joseph Delaney writes. I'm so excited for the new series!'

Daniella Wilson

'A couple of years ago I used to hate books. My mum on the other hand was a keen reader, and she gave me the first book in the series and told me to try it. Just a few pages in, I could not put it down. I never thought I could get so much enjoyment from a book. Nor did I believe I could become so attached to its characters! When I first stumbled across Alice, there was something about her that intrigued me. The fact that Alice was a healer made me wonder if "healers" were real. So, I hit the internet. And I spent page after page reading about real-life healers. Now I too have become a healer, just like Alice. Her character inspired me so much that I realized there was something missing from my life. Joseph introduced me to the magical world of books and reading. Alice helped me find my path. Thank you, Joseph. Thank you, Alice. I can't wait to get stuck into the new book!'

Emily Critchley

'When I first read *The Spook's Apprentice*, it was a dark time in my young life, and I hadn't read a book for enjoyment in years. My friend offered me his copy while on a camping trip. While everyone was asleep, I had my light on at my little bunk, reading for hours! I couldn't put it down. Mr Delaney reinvigorated my love of reading. I've felt more at home in the Spook's house than I did in my own home sometimes. So I would like to give a big thank-you to Mr Delaney. You've inspired me and so many others with your writing. Never stop, good sir!'

Michael Reeder

'The Spooks series is so creative – they are the reason I started writing and all my inspiration derives from them. I literally read a book a day!'

Thomas Stacey

PUFFIN BOOKS

BROTHER WULF

Also available by Joseph Delaney

THE SPOOK'S SERIES
The Spook's Apprentice
The Spook's Curse
The Spook's Secret
The Spook's Battle
The Spook's Mistake
The Spook's Sacrifice
The Spook's Nightmare
The Spook's Destiny
I Am Grimalkin
The Spook's Blood
Slither's Tale
Alice
The Spook's Revenge

The Spook's Stories: Witches
The Spook's Bestiary

The Seventh Apprentice
A New Darkness
The Dark Army
Dark Assassin

ARENA 13 SERIES
Arena 13
The Prey
The Warrior

ABERRATIONS SERIES
The Beast Awakens
The Witch's Warning

JOSEPH DELANEY

BROTHER WULF

PUFFIN

PUFFIN BOOKS

UK | USA | Canada | Ireland | Australia
India | New Zealand | South Africa

Puffin Books is part of the Penguin Random House group of companies
whose addresses can be found at global.penguinrandomhouse.com.

www.penguin.co.uk
www.puffin.co.uk
www.ladybird.co.uk

Penguin
Random House
UK

First published 2020

001

Text copyright © Joseph Delaney, 2020
Map illustration by Alessia Trunfio

The moral right of the author has been asserted

Set in 10/16.5 pt Palatino LT Std
Typeset by Jouve (UK), Milton Keynes
Printed and bound in Great Britain by Clays Ltd, Elcograf S.p.A.

A CIP catalogue record for this book is available from the British Library

ISBN: 978–0–241–41649–5

All correspondence to:
Puffin Books
Penguin Random House Children's
80 Strand, London WC2R ORL

For Marie

Prologue

I could no longer see my bedroom ceiling. The room had suddenly grown dark, as if a thick blanket had been thrown over my face. I couldn't even see my breath.

I panicked and tried to sit up, but I was frozen. Then all at once I was able to see again – though I soon wished I couldn't.

The ceiling gave out a faint, sickly yellow light, and against it I could see a moving pattern of darkness. At first it looked like the flickering shadows cast upon the ground by moonlight passing through the branches of a leafless tree. But soon those shadows took on a distinct form. It was a human figure made of sticks – but it had no face.

By now my palms were sweating and my heart was racing. I was truly afraid. I tried in vain to look away.

Then something spoke to me. It was a deep and terrifying voice that vibrated through my teeth and echoed back from the walls. It was not the voice of a human being. Only a demon could sound like that.

'*You will obey me! You will do everything I command. Do you understand?*'

I was a young noviciate monk, training to serve the Church. I should not be doing the will of a demon. I opened my mouth to refuse, but before I could reply the demon spoke again.

'*If you do not do my bidding, you will suffer. You will suffer terrible pain. Pain such as this!*'

It seared right through my body from head to toe. My muscles locked and then convulsed. I gasped in agony.

'Please! Please!' I cried. 'Please stop, I beg you!'

The pain went on. The demon was without mercy.

I was in its power.

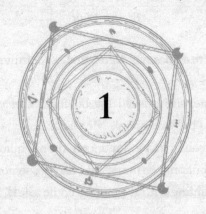

THE WITHY TREES

Thunder crashed and devil lightning forked above me as I trudged up the achingly steep hill towards Chipenden village. Grey clouds cloaked the tops of the fells, and I knew that rain would soon follow the warning sounds of the thunderstorm. It would be dark in less than an hour too, and I dreaded to think what that would mean for me, a lone traveller in the County . . .

I shivered, and picked up my pace. When I finally reached the village's cobbled streets, I swiftly entered the first shop I saw. Two large pigs' heads were positioned at each end of a long, blood-stained wooden counter like bookends. But this was certainly no library. Rather than leather-bound tomes, between the heads was a long row of pork chops. A big man stood behind the counter, eyeing me suspiciously. It seemed they didn't welcome strangers here. But never mind that, I told myself – I was on a mission.

'Excuse me, sir,' I asked the butcher. 'Can you tell me where to find the local spook, Mr Ward?'

The man stared at me for a long time while wiping his hands on his apron. 'And what would someone of your calling be wanting with a spook, boy?' he asked, looking me up and down.

I knew I must have appeared somewhat strange. I was a noviciate – a monk in my first year of training – and my clothing made that plain for all to see. My habit consisted of a black tunic tied at the waist with a leather belt and fitted with a hood. Additionally I wore an overshirt that indicated my lowly position. Priests don't usually have dealings with spooks. We don't hold with their methods – the way in which they confront the dark without the use of prayer and meditation – and think it an unholy business. For that reason, most won't even allow a dead spook to be buried on holy ground. So I could understand why my question might seem peculiar.

'I'm here on behalf of someone who needs his help very badly,' I replied.

'Help against the dark?' the butcher asked, resting his elbows on the blood-stained counter.

I nodded, not wishing to go into detail. For two days I'd been hurrying to Chipenden as fast as I could, and I couldn't waste time on questions like this. I needed to find this spook as soon as possible.

'You mean to say you couldn't sort out the problem with prayer? Well, that does surprise me!' the butcher said, his voice full of sarcasm. 'What's causing the trouble – a boggart?'

'No, sir. It's a witch,' I explained, trying to stay calm and contain my impatience.

The butcher laughed out loud at that, though I couldn't see anything funny about it. Witches were powerful, dangerous – and all too real, as I had discovered recently.

However, the man finally led me outside and pointed up the deserted street.

'There's a lane leads north out of the village towards a big house standing amid some trees. That's where the Spook lives. But don't go up the path if you value your life – it's guarded by a savage boggart that will rip you to pieces as soon as you enter the garden. Instead, take the narrow track to the northeast. It'll bring you to a crossroads beneath a stand of willow trees. You'll find a bell hanging there. Ring it, and the Spook will come out to you. That's assuming he's not away on business. If he is, you might have a very long wait indeed.'

I listened carefully, but wasn't sure that the butcher had his facts right. I knew that boggarts were dangerous: spooks hunted them down and killed them. So why would one guard a spook's house and garden? It seemed very unlikely.

'Thank you for your help,' I said dubiously, and set off up the street, glad to be away at last. Then, after a few seconds, I heard a shout and turned back.

'Hey!' the butcher yelled, and I saw him grinning. 'Do witches scare you, boy?'

I nodded. It was the truth.

'Well, be prepared to be scared some more. There's something you should know about our local spook – he lives with a witch!'

Now I was *sure* he had to be joking, so I smiled politely, turned my back and hurried on my way. Everyone knew that spooks were the enemies of witches. They certainly wouldn't share a house with one!

I struggled on as fast as I could. I was tired out, having walked all the way from Salford, which was a long way off in the south of the County, and my legs felt like lead. In view of what had happened, I thought I was probably already too late to bring help – but I'd promised myself that I would at least try. And I always keep my promises.

I didn't like the look of the crossroads when I reached it. As the butcher had told me, it was cloaked by big willow trees with drooping branches that hung almost to the ground. The whole area was very gloomy, and I realized that it would soon be dark. The storm seemed to have passed by; it was very quiet here – as if something was lurking nearby, silencing all the birds and animals.

I didn't like that eerie silence. I didn't like it one bit.

I could see the rope hanging down so, wasting no time, I gave it a tug. The peal of noise from the bell above shattered the silence, and soon I was pulling it rhythmically, just as I did when it was my turn to join the bell ringers at the abbey. After about five minutes of ringing, there was still no response, so I stopped for a short rest. Where was the Spook? I wondered. I really hoped he was at home . . .

Just as I was about to start ringing again, a hooded figure carrying a staff appeared among the trees, heading towards me. I gulped. Was this the Spook? I assumed so.

He stopped about five paces away and pulled back his hood. I was shocked by his youthful appearance. He couldn't have been older than nineteen or twenty. Maybe this was just the Spook's apprentice . . .

'Greetings. Are you Mr Ward, the Spook?' I asked tentatively.

'I am. What's your business?' The man was tall and dark-haired, and there was not an ounce of fat on him. Although well worn, his black cloak was of good-quality material, far superior to my habit. He wore neat grey breeches, but I was particularly impressed by his boots, which were made of the very best leather. It seemed that being a spook paid well. However, the man's pleasant face was set in a stern expression. He didn't seem unfriendly, merely brusque and business-like. I wondered if it was because he was talking to a noviciate monk – after all, we don't often find ourselves on the same side . . .

I screwed up my courage, and told him the reason why I had come. 'I'm here to ask for your help with a very dangerous witch. I was with another spook down south, but when he tried to deal with her, everything went wrong. Now he's fallen into her hands, and I fear for his life. I feel that it's my duty to try and help him. As he'd mentioned your name, I came here as quickly as I could.'

The Spook frowned. 'Where did this happen?'

'Just south of Salford. It's taken me over two days to get here,' I explained.

'And what's this spook's name?' he asked.

'Spook Johnson.'

'Yes, I've heard of him. I believe he was once apprenticed to my own master, John Gregory. What were *you* doing in the company of a spook anyway?' Mr Ward asked. 'You look more like a young monk than an apprentice. What do they call you?'

'You're right. I'm not his apprentice,' I admitted. 'I'm a noviciate nearing the end of my first year of training at Kersal Abbey in Salford. My name is Brother Beowulf and I've been working for Spook Johnson as a scribe.'

'What does he need a scribe for?' Mr Ward asked, looking puzzled. 'He must be able to read and write or he wouldn't be a spook. An apprentice doesn't get taken on without some basic skills.'

'He can write – but not half as well as I can.'

Mr Ward smiled at that. Now he looked much more friendly, and I felt sure he would help me.

'It's a long story,' I explained. 'I'll tell you all about it on the journey there.'

He nodded. 'Fine, I'll come. Sounds like whatever it is you're dealing with is serious. However, it's getting dark now, and there's heavy rain on the way, so we'll set off in the morning.'

I hadn't expected this. Given that one of his brother spooks was in danger, I'd expected him to come at once. Perhaps I hadn't been clear enough.

'We should go now,' I urged him. 'There's no time to lose!'

'I've told you – there's no way I'm wandering about in the dark with a novice monk when there's a storm setting in. It's not worth the risk. We'll set off tomorrow at dawn. Now follow me – you can sleep up at the house.'

'I don't want to sleep and neither should you!' I protested, raising my voice a little without meaning to. What didn't this man understand? 'Spook Johnson might be dead if we wait until morning.'

The Spook took a step towards me and glowered. 'You listen to me,' he said, an edge of anger in his voice. 'I will go and do my best for Spook Johnson, but *I'm* the one who'll decide when and how. I'm the Spook here. Do you understand?'

I nodded, suddenly afraid.

'He might be dead already, Brother Beowulf,' he continued, his voice softening. 'Besides, you look worn out. Get a good night's sleep – tomorrow I'll be setting a good pace and taking few rests.'

The Spook turned without waiting for an answer, and strode off through the trees and up the hill. I trotted after him, but it was hard to keep up. If this was the pace he'd talked about, I would certainly need all the sleep I could get!

Up ahead I could see a hawthorn hedge with a gap in it. This seemed to mark the edge of the garden. Beyond it I could see long grass and trees, and then a big house, dark against the fading light. But before we got there I heard a warning growl; it sounded deeper and more threatening than a dog. Some dangerous beast was lurking there in the darkness of the trees. It made the hairs on the back of my neck stand up and my knees started to wobble.

The butcher had warned me about a boggart, but I'd dismissed that as casually as his other joke about Mr Ward living with a witch. Spooks hunted boggarts and destroyed them, didn't they? I thought. They wouldn't keep them close. But now I felt a chill that told me that the danger ahead was real. I'd encountered a boggart before and knew that they could kill.

The Spook came to a halt. 'Stand still,' he told me softly.

I obeyed, and he went round behind me, put down his staff and placed both hands on my shoulders.

'Kratch! Kratch! Kratch! Listen well!' he called out in a loud voice. 'This boy is under my protection. Harm not a hair of his head while he is within the boundaries that you control!'

There was another low growl, but this time it sounded further away. Then there was silence. So it really *had* been a boggart! I realized. Mr Ward had called out *Kratch* – it even had a name!

'The butcher told me that a boggart guarded your garden, but I didn't believe him,' I cried in astonishment.

'Yes, it guards the garden and even makes breakfast!' Mr Ward laughed as we moved on.

Surely *that* had to be a joke – a domesticated boggart? I couldn't imagine what strange sights I might see next at this odd house. And I was rather afraid to find out.

We left the trees and walked through the knee-high grass of a big lawn to reach what seemed to be the back door of the house. I glanced upwards and saw that it was three storeys high, with several windows on both upper floors. It was large enough to accommodate half a dozen spooks – and I wondered if Mr Ward was lonely, here all by himself. Well, apart from the boggart, of course . . .

It was very gloomy now, and a single flickering yellow light from a downstairs window illuminated a strip of the garden. The door was unlocked. No doubt with a boggart about there was no need to fear burglars. I followed the Spook into a small room, keeping my eyes peeled for strange things. I still didn't trust this man – or his house. He took off his cloak and hung it on a hook by the door and leaned his staff in the corner. Underneath the cloak he was wearing a black tunic. Black seemed to be his favourite colour, I noted wryly. It certainly wasn't mine. I wore that colour too, but not by choice – it was the traditional habit of a monk.

'No doubt you're hungry,' Mr Ward said with a smile, and opened the door to what seemed to be the kitchen, beckoning me to follow. I gave a small gasp, for it was a sight to delight the eye. The flagged room was warm and inviting, with a big blazing fire warming the whole space. It was also very bright, with a row of candles lighting the mantelpiece. It all looked very homely – there were even herbs in pots on the window ledge. In fact, it brought back some of my earliest happy memories as I watched my mother prepare meals. The abbey was a terribly cold and cheerless place after my cosy home.

I spotted food on the large oak table too. A tureen of steaming pea soup, some cheese, and freshly baked bread. My stomach growled loudly, and reminded me that I hadn't eaten properly for days.

I sat down eagerly; Mr Ward filled our bowls to the brim and we ate in silence. The soup was delicious. At first I sipped it – it was very hot. Then, as it cooled, I ladled it quickly into my mouth. Finally I soaked up the remainder with the warm bread until not a drop remained. The Spook chuckled as I wolfed it down.

'Did the boggart make the soup?' I asked, attempting a joke of my own.

'No, it only makes breakfast. Alice made this. I'm sorry she's not here to greet you but she's not feeling too well and has gone to bed early.'

My heart lurched. Was Alice the witch the butcher had warned me about? I couldn't believe it. How could anyone – let alone a spook – live with a witch?

'Is Alice your housekeeper?' I ventured.

The Spook shook his head. 'No, she's' – he eyed me carefully – 'a very close friend of mine.'

I was a little shocked at that. Witch or not, unless they were related or married, it wasn't proper for a man and a woman to share the same house. I consoled myself with another slice of bread with some cheese. It was my favourite – crumbly County cheese, something we only rarely ate at the monastery.

'Well, if you're quite done eating me out of house and home, I'll show you up to your room,' the Spook said wryly, coming to his feet.

Even though he was clearly joking, I blushed, then followed him out of the kitchen and up a narrow winding staircase to the first landing. He approached a door which was painted green and pushed it open, handing a candle to me.

'We'll set off soon after dawn, so at first light you'll hear a bell ring downstairs. That's the summons to come down for breakfast. No doubt you'll be used to that, being a monk and all ... But don't come down before then!' he warned seriously. 'The boggart doesn't like being disturbed while it's preparing breakfast.'

Now I saw that there wasn't even a flicker of humour on his face. He clearly meant every word of what he'd said – though I still couldn't quite believe that a boggart could make breakfast ...

After he'd gone, I placed the candle on the bedside table and looked about me. There were fresh sheets on a single bed which stood next to a sash window. Rain was battering the small panes of glass, running down the outside in rivulets. It looked like that storm had finally broken.

It was then that the wall at the foot of the bed caught my attention. The other three walls had clean white plaster but this one was old and cracked and tainted with smoke. I picked up the candle again and moved closer to examine it.

Somebody had been writing on it. No – not just one person. There were lots of names in different handwriting, maybe thirty or more, some written in large bold letters, others small and squeezed into the available spaces. Each was a signature.

Why had they written their names here? I peered closer. Some were really hard to read. One of the names was relatively clear but quite small.

Billy Bradley

I wondered how long ago he'd scrawled his name on the wall and what he was doing now.

Then another name caught my eye:

William Johnson

Suddenly I understood. Spook Johnson, the man I was sworn to rescue, must have written that when he lived in this house. These were the names of all the apprentices who'd been trained here. They must have slept in this bedroom, one by one, over the course of many years.

All were boys' names except one . . .

Jenny

I frowned. Was that yet another joke? A spook having a girl apprentice was even more unlikely than having a female priest! Everyone knew that, in order to be a spook, you needed to be the seventh son of a seventh son – even if we in the Church dismissed it as superstitious nonsense.

I was suddenly bone-achingly tired, so I blew out the candle and crawled into bed, listening to the rain. I thought of Spook Johnson, in the clutches of the witch. I felt bad lying here safe and warm while he was probably suffering or dead.

Still, I'd done my best for him, I told myself. I could have simply gone straight back to the abbey, and left him to his fate – the Abbot wouldn't have blamed me for that. In fact, he'd probably have preferred it. He'd ordered me to become Johnson's scribe, but that was as far as the relationship went. However, I was troubled, and felt a little guilty.

It took me a long time to get to sleep.

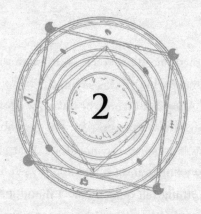

2

COMPLIMENTS TO THE CHEF

I woke suddenly, startled by the sound of some kind of argument between a man and a woman. It was still the middle of the night, and pitch black in my room – but I could hear yelling, clear as day.

I listened carefully. It was the woman who was doing the shouting. The male voice was lower and seemed to be trying to reason with her. Was Mr Ward arguing with the one he'd called Alice? The one I feared was the witch the butcher had warned me about?

Unless there was someone else living in the house, it had to be, I thought.

Then, quite distinctly, I heard her call out: 'Not now! Not now! What kind of a man are you? How can you be so cruel?'

I was puzzled. What could they be arguing about that was so terrible? The woman sounded desperate, and very upset.

Mr Ward then raised his voice a little so that, for the first time, I could hear what he was saying.

'I'm *sorry*, Alice, but I'll only be away for a few days – it's my duty to go. How can I refuse?'

'Your duty is to stay with me, Tom. That should be as plain as the nose on your face.'

Soon everything fell quiet again. I thought I could hear crying, but maybe it was just the rain driving against the window. Eventually I fell asleep again.

I was awoken again a few hours later by the distant sound of a bell and leaped out of bed immediately. Mr Ward was right – the routine of the abbey certainly gets you used to pre-dawn starts. I dressed hurriedly. I was famished and didn't want my breakfast to grow cold.

And what a breakfast it proved to be!

The tantalizing aroma of food drew me back down the stairs, and into the large flagged kitchen.

'Sit down and tuck in!' invited Mr Ward, who was already at the table. 'That's all we'll eat before nightfall. I don't intend to stop on the way.'

I didn't need a second invitation. There were two large dishes laden with bacon and sausages, and three fried eggs on my plate. There was also a freshly baked loaf, and butter to spread on it. This would have sufficed for four monks! It was a feast fit for the Abbot himself!

I eagerly helped myself to bacon and sausages. They were steaming hot – and delicious! In the refectory at the abbey, we noviciates were always the last to be served and the food was often barely warm.

For a while neither of us spoke, both too busy eating. I paused only to butter myself another hunk of bread, which was also delicious. I wondered where Mr Ward's 'close friend' Alice was, but I thought it best not to enquire after what I'd heard last night. Suddenly I was aware of the sound of purring. It came from the hearthrug, and I turned towards it in puzzlement.

Then, to my astonishment, something began to materialize there, and I stopped chewing. It was a large ginger cat with only one eye. All that remained of the other was a vertical scar.

'Don't stare at it,' the Spook advised, not looking up from his plate of food. 'It's best to carry on eating and pretend you haven't noticed it. Boggarts don't like being watched.'

'Is this the boggart that made the breakfast?' I asked, my voice hardly more than a whisper. 'How could it do that? It hasn't any hands!'

'Well, as you may know, boggarts are mostly invisible,' Mr Ward replied. 'However, they sometimes take on the shape of animals, and this is what's known as a *cat-boggart* – though that shape is only what it chooses to reveal to humans. On my first morning at this house as an apprentice I made the big mistake of coming downstairs too early. I entered the kitchen while the boggart was still preparing breakfast. It was invisible, and it gave me a tremendous clout on the back of the head. I'll never forget it – though it could have been worse! So don't be fooled – what you see purring before the fire is not its true shape.'

I nodded and looked away. It didn't look very dangerous, I thought – more like a family pet.

'What does it do to people who enter your garden uninvited?' I asked. 'The butcher down in the village said it could rip you into pieces.'

Mr Ward nodded. 'He wasn't exaggerating. It can, and has done so in the past. But it gives warning howls which scare most people off. And the locals know better than to come anywhere near this house and garden. That's why I have the bell at the withy trees.'

He pushed his plate away and gave a sigh. Something about the way he did so suggested that he was unhappy. I guessed he was thinking about the argument last night, and I wondered why the woman had been so desperate not to be left alone. Surely a spook must travel a lot and be away for days at a time. Surely she must have got used to the Spook's comings and goings by now? But for how long had she been his friend?

Maybe this was the first time he'd left her alone and she was scared to be in the house with such a dangerous boggart?

'Had your fill of food?' Mr Ward asked, interrupting my thoughts.

I nodded. 'Thanks for the bed and my breakfast,' I replied.

He smiled. 'You should thank the boggart for the latter,' he said. 'Never mind – I'll do it for both of us!'

He turned his chair away from the table so that he was facing the large ginger cat. 'Our compliments to the chef!' he cried. 'That was an excellent breakfast, cooked to perfection.'

The cat-boggart began to purr even more loudly – and then it simply disappeared. I gaped in astonishment.

'Right, let's be on our way,' Mr Ward said, grinning at my baffled face and rising to his feet.

I thought he might take leave of his friend, Alice, but I saw no sign of her as we gathered our things together, and within minutes we were striding away from the house. Perhaps they're not so friendly after all, I thought – though Mr Ward's grim-looking face suggested that something wasn't quite right.

And indeed we'd almost reached the hawthorn hedge that marked the garden's boundary when the Spook suddenly came to a halt.

'Sorry, Brother Beowulf, but I've forgotten something. I just need to go back to the house. Wait here. I won't be long.'

More delays! I was impatient to be off and, when he hadn't returned after a couple of minutes, I started to grow annoyed. After pacing backwards and forwards for another long minute, I gathered my courage and marched back through the trees towards the house.

Then I saw him and came to a halt.

The Spook was standing near the door of the house with his back towards me. He had his arms wrapped around someone. I was too far away to make her out properly, but I could see she was young, with dark hair, and she had her hands on his shoulders.

Fearing to be seen – I didn't want the Spook to think I'd been spying on him – I quickly turned away and walked back to the hawthorn hedge. Almost immediately Mr Ward came striding through the trees towards me. Without a word between us we set off on our journey.

From what I'd seen, he'd ended the quarrel with his friend. However, judging by the sad expression on his face, it hadn't made him any happier.

We walked all day, at a fast pace with hardly a pause for breath, let alone any talking. The Spook carried both his staff and his heavy bag. At least he didn't expect me to deal with that, as Johnson did! There wasn't much to do except look around and take in the scenery – and late in the afternoon I thought I saw a woman watching us from a distance. I dismissed it as tiredness, but after the sun began to go down and the gloom intensified, I twice glimpsed movements out of the corner of my eye. Now I was certain that we were being followed.

Soon darkness fell, and we finally stopped. Supper was meagre – a far cry from the night before: the Spook merely offered me a few pieces of County cheese. It was very tasty, but my belly went on rumbling. The fire was burning low and I kept glancing nervously into the darkness. We were in a clearing surrounded by trees. I didn't think it was a good place to camp for the night.

'I think we're being followed,' I told Mr Ward.

'You're right, Brother Beowulf. We are.'

I was surprised to discover how calm he was. 'I think it's a woman,' I said. 'Earlier today I saw her among the trees, staring down at us. I wasn't sure if she was real – she was tall, and she looked angry. No, it was worse than that. She looked furious, as if she hated the whole world.'

'That's an accurate description of Makrilda,' he agreed, and surprised me again by smiling.

'Do you know the woman?' I asked.

'We met once. She's the witch assassin of the Malkin clan – the strongest of the witch clans that surround Pendle. When they want somebody dead, she does the killing.'

'I didn't even know witches had clans,' I told the Spook with a frown. 'Why is she following us? Do they want *you* dead?'

'I'm not sure. I think Makrilda's probably just stalking me on her own initiative. If she gets the chance, she'll slit my throat and take my thumbs to wear around her neck. Bone witches use them to gain dark magical power, you see.'

'*She'd wear your thumbs around her neck?*' I said, horrified.

Mr Ward nodded. 'Afraid so. And spooks' thumb-bones are particularly valuable to them.'

'So she sees you as an enemy because you're a spook?'

'Oh, it's a bit more than that,' he chuckled. 'It's personal. We once had a bit of a scrap and I won. That was bad enough, but many of her clan were witnesses to her defeat. Her pride's hurt, so she needs to kill me to save face. If she can show them my thumb-bones, she'll feel a lot better.'

'You don't seem very worried . . .'

He shrugged. 'Being a spook is a dangerous job – you get used to living with threats like that. Besides, she's followed me lots of times before without doing anything but watch. She'll be gone soon enough.'

'What if it's different this time? What if she tries to kill you tonight? Or maybe tomorrow?' Spook Ward may have been calm about the idea of a witch assassin watching us, but I certainly wasn't.

'To succeed in killing me, she'd need to be very lucky!' he said, and grinned again. I flinched a little. Until that moment he'd seemed benign and polite, but now I glimpsed something feral and dangerous in his eyes. For a moment he looked almost wolfish.

'So would you kill *her*?' I asked. 'Why don't you just kill her now, if it's so easy?'

'Because it would achieve nothing. The clan would simply choose another witch assassin, who would no doubt come after me too. And don't get me wrong – these are very dangerous witches who thrive on combat. They enjoy killing. They also have a cruel way of selecting new assassins. The candidates fight it out one by one, to the death, and the one still alive at the end becomes the new assassin.'

I shuddered, imagining the carnage.

The Spook continued, seemingly unfazed. 'So there will always be a Malkin assassin, which means it's always going to be a factor for a spook working in the County. I once formed a useful alliance with their previous assassin, but that was very unusual. She was called Grimalkin, and we fought common enemies. We developed a way of working together.' For a moment he looked grim. 'But she's dead now.'

I nodded. 'So you'd like to form another modus operandi with this one?'

He smiled again. 'A modus operandi . . . I don't often hear Latin any more. My mother taught me the language – that and a little Greek. My master continued to teach me as part of my training.'

'I'm studying Latin, but I'm not very good at it,' I admitted. 'I try to use words whenever I can. We monks obviously need Latin to say our prayers, but how does Latin help a spook? You don't use spells, do you? Spook Johnson never did.'

Mr Ward shook his head. 'We don't use spells. Being a spook is a craft, a trade with practical skills that have to be learned and honed. But witches often use Latin in their spells, so it's good to be able to understand what they're up to.'

I nodded. Perhaps we monks had more in common with spooks than I'd thought.

Then Mr Ward abruptly changed the subject. 'I think the time has come for you to tell me exactly what happened with the witch. Let's start at the beginning. Why did Spook Johnson decide he wanted a scribe?'

His tone seemed friendly enough, but there was an edge to it.

I sat up straight. If I was going to be interrogated, I needed to have my wits about me. 'Johnson is vain. He's concerned the people of Salford don't think much of him, so he wanted a record of his exploits as a spook, to show people what he's achieved.'

Mr Ward narrowed his eyes. 'And why do you think the good folk of Salford take such a dim view of him?'

I hesitated, but it wasn't in me to lie. 'He's somewhat . . . over-zealous in his pursuit of witches. People believe that some of the witches he imprisons in pits are innocent.'

'And what do *you* think?'

'I couldn't say. I don't know that much about witches. But people sometimes curse him in the street – though only from a distance. You really wouldn't want to do it up close. He's big and he has a nasty temper . . .' I paused, considering what to say next carefully. 'I think the ones who dislike him most are those who have family members in his clutches. If he'd taken your wife, mother or daughter, you wouldn't be very happy, would you?'

Mr Ward nodded and gave me a very hard stare. 'I'm going to ask you something and I want you to tell me the truth. I can understand why Spook Johnson might want to have a scribe to make him look better to the world than perhaps he is. But the Church doesn't hold with spooks – and we don't hold with you. So how is it that you ended up working for Spook Johnson?'

I swallowed. There was no way to avoid it. I had to tell the truth – or at least *most* of the truth.

3

THE NOVICIATE'S TALE

While I was considering what to say, I remembered the night
before it all started. It had been very bad. I hadn't slept at all.
The voices had been whispering in my ears, and once I'd felt
cold fingers gently stroking my brow.

I'd been plagued like this for as long as I could remember.
My dad used to beat me, claiming I made up stories about
ghosts and the like; he said it wasn't fair to keep the whole
family awake with my screams. When he died in an accident
on the farm, I tried to keep quiet for my poor mother's sake –
especially when I saw his ghost skulking around the barn.
More than once she came into my room while I was crying.

As I grew older, I was still tortured during the night. It was
my mother's idea that I should become a monk. She said it
would help me get nearer to God, and that all the praying in
the abbey would keep the Devil and his creatures away.

But so far it hadn't worked. In fact, things had got worse.

However, I decided not to tell Spook Ward about the voices. There were some things that I liked to keep to myself.

After that particularly awful night I went into the chapel for matins, hardly able to keep my eyes open. I was kneeling, shivering there on the cold flags, trying to concentrate on my prayers, when Brother Halsall walked across and whispered in my ear – and this is where I started my tale for Mr Ward.

'The Abbot wants to speak to you. Go at once!' he hissed.

My heart fluttered in my chest as I did as he bade me. The Abbot had never spoken a word to me before. What did he want now? I wondered. Brother Halsall was a big, irascible bear of a man; he was the monk in charge of noviciates. He was strict and nothing escaped his attention. Which meant that nothing I did ever pleased him. Had he reported me for something? What if someone had heard me crying out during the night?

Full of trepidation, I knocked on the door of the Abbot's room and he bade me enter. I walked in to find him seated on a large red velvet chair, sneezing into a handkerchief that was stained with yellow streaks. There were two small chairs in addition to his own, but he didn't invite me to sit down.

Kersal Abbey was cold and draughty through autumn, winter, spring, and even now in the latter part of the summer, but here, in the Abbot's room, it was warm. There was a big fire in the grate with sparks flying up the chimney. The Abbot had the best of everything. He was a man who liked his food, and he always got the very best, specially prepared and brought to his room on silver dishes. Rumour had it that there was always enough food heaped on his plate to satisfy half a dozen monks. Whether that was true or not, he clearly wasn't starving. He had a florid face and a large paunch, which I found myself staring at. I couldn't imagine being lucky enough to get so fat!

'Brother Beowulf,' the Abbot said, and I started, bringing my attention back to my interview. 'Generally I have received good reports of your progress. The brothers tell me that you are an excellent scribe.'

This was completely unexpected and I didn't know what to say.

'Thank you, Father,' I muttered.

'I am told that your writing is pleasing to the eye and that you copy with great accuracy. However, there is one thing for which you have been reprimanded more than once . . .'

I hung my head in shame. I knew what was coming next. Now this summoning made sense.

'On two occasions Brother Halsall has caught you creating your own narratives. Writing your *own stories* – such sin! Do you not know that such works of the imagination must eventually lead to irresistible temptations? Imagination belongs to *God*. It is not for us poor humans to attempt to exercise that faculty. On top of this, you have wasted precious paper! Explain yourself immediately, boy.'

I flushed a deep scarlet, and kept my head bowed low. 'I am truly sorry, Father. They were just short accounts of my life at the abbey. I . . . I recorded things so that one day, in the future, I might look back on them and recall my memories of this . . . *happy* time . . . with more ease and accuracy.'

The Abbot shook his head, and frowned deeply at me. 'There is a terrible danger in what you have done, Brother. However, I think we can put your abilities to a use that might cause God to forgive such a trespass.' I looked up, surprised. The Abbot continued. 'There is a spook who operates in this area. His name is Johnson and it seems he has need of a scribe. He is prepared to pay good money into the abbey coffers in exchange for the work. He has specified certain criteria that the scribe must meet. You are the only monk, noviciate though you be, who meets his full requirements. Therefore you will become his scribe until such a time as the work has been completed.'

I was astonished by his words. The Church considered the work of spooks to be an unholy business – though I knew that people from my village considered them effective. They got rid of creatures from Hell such as boggarts, ghosts and witches – and although most ordinary folk were nervous of being around spooks, they were only too happy to seek their help.

In fact, when I was a child a spook had once sorted out a problem on a neighbouring farm. Something had been screaming in the night and killing cattle. One visit from a spook and the problem had gone away. So the more I thought about it, the less daunted I felt by the idea of becoming a scribe for a spook. It would at least make a change from the routines at the abbey. And who knew – perhaps he could help me with my problem too . . .

'Does he wish me to copy a book, Father?' I said, curious to know what would be asked of me.

'No, Brother Beowulf. He wants you to write an account of his exploits as a spook, which are to be recorded for posterity. What he wishes is foolish and vain – another sin to add to those which must surely drag him down to Hell . . .'

'But I don't understand, Father. Won't I be sinning too in joining him in this enterprise?' I asked, confused.

'We will find a suitable penance for you on your return,' the Abbot said dismissively. Then he paused, and lowered his voice. 'Besides, unknown to him, you will have another role – and if you carry it out successfully, that will furnish you with grace enough to outweigh sin and balance the scales in your favour. We want you to discover all his secrets and dark practices. For too long spooks have been allowed to flourish without check. And, as you know, we have a new Bishop of Blackburn who has declared his firm intention to cleanse the County of spooks. We are therefore gathering evidence on all those who practise that vile trade, usurping the mission of the Church. And, unwittingly, Spook Johnson has played right into our hands.'

The Abbot rubbed his hands in satisfaction and I gave a weak smile. I didn't like the idea of being a spy. It could be dangerous. What if the Spook caught me at it? However, I could not refuse an order from the Abbot.

'So you want me to record my findings, Father?'

He frowned and looked me straight in the eye. 'Don't risk writing them down in case Spook Johnson discovers your notes. Brother Halsall tells me that you have an excellent memory,' he said. 'Use that gift from God to store what you learn. No doubt the Spook will condemn himself from his own lips as he gives you the details to write his memoir. What we discover about this spook will be used against all spooks. You will be a witness at their trials before the Holy Courts. I predict that, with your help, within a year all of them will have been burned at the stake . . .'

I could feel Mr Ward staring at me, but his face was in shadow and I couldn't read the expression in his eyes.

'So you were being sent to spy on Spook Johnson?' he asked me.

I nodded and opened my mouth to explain myself further, but he stopped me by raising his hand, palm towards me.

'And you knew that what you found would be used in evidence and would lead to spooks being burned at the stake?' he went on.

This time he lowered his hand, permitting me to reply.

'I didn't have much choice, Mr Ward. When the Abbot tells you to do something, you do it,' I explained.

He laughed grimly, then considered me further. 'I asked you for the truth, Brother Beowulf, and you've given it to me – indeed, it strikes me that you've gone much further than I would have expected. There was no need for you to tell me about the Abbot's plan, was there? You could have held that back.'

I sighed, and pushed my confession even further. 'I wanted you to have a full account. But there was another reason. Recently a lot of my thinking has changed. I . . . I have decided I no longer wish to become a monk. Whether we manage to save Johnson or not, I won't be going back to the abbey. So you needn't worry about any report that I might make.'

'I see,' said Mr Ward, clearly surprised by my answer. 'What will you do then? How will you feed yourself?'

I shrugged. I had been wondering this too. 'I was raised on a farm but I can't go back there. My father and mother are both dead. My mother died in the third month of my noviciate . . .'

I paused, halted by that sad and bitter memory. After I'd heard the news, Brother Halsall came to tell me that the

Abbot had refused permission for me to go home for the funeral. Apparently the Church was my family now and I could pray for her more effectively here in the abbey.

I was still angry about it, but I took a deep breath and continued. 'My eldest brother works the farm now. I wouldn't be welcome – it hardly supports his family as it is. But I do know something about farming. Maybe I could get a job as a farmhand.'

The Spook nodded thoughtfully. Then he came slowly to his feet, stretched and yawned.

'That's enough for tonight. You can tell me what happened to Spook Johnson tomorrow – it'll keep for the journey to Salford. Now try and get some sleep if you can. But just one thing . . .'

I clambered to my feet and stared at him expectantly, waiting for him to finish.

'If you hear a scream in the night, don't worry. It'll probably just be me killing the witch.'

It was too dark to tell whether he was smiling or not. Was it his idea of a joke or was he being serious?

As usual, it took me a long time to get to sleep. Only this time it wasn't just fear of the nightmares that kept me awake.

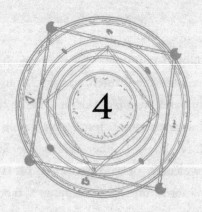

4

SOME SLIMY ABOMINATION

The next morning I felt stiff and cold and there was no cooked breakfast – just another morsel of crumbly cheese that the Spook handed me from his bag.

We set off at a brisk pace, but just as I'd started to warm up and feel better it began to rain. It wasn't the torrential rain that had lashed Chipenden two days earlier. This was a cold, miserable, incessant drizzle that soon soaked me to the bone.

But Mr Ward continued his relentless march south, if anything increasing his pace so that I struggled to keep up. At noon I assumed we'd rest and eat.

And we did: we paused for five minutes and ate another morsel of cheese standing up in the drizzle. Mr Ward didn't even bother to seek shelter under a tree.

On we went through the afternoon. I knew we were heading towards Salford, but this wasn't the route I'd taken when travelling north to find the Spook. However, he seemed to know exactly where he was. I was lagging behind now, and he waved me forward to catch up.

'Will we reach Salford before dark?' I asked as I drew alongside him.

'No. Just beyond the next rise is a village called Pendlebury,' he told me. 'I don't often do this when I'm about spook's business, but I can see that you're exhausted. We're going to stay at an inn. There'll be a hot supper and a warm dry bed for the night. It's best if we're rested. Tomorrow, sometime before noon, we'll be going up against your witch.'

'*We?*' I asked, terrified at the thought of what that might involve. 'You want me to help?'

The Spook gave me that wolfish grin again. 'Perhaps you're right. Maybe you should just watch and take notes in your head – remember what you see. What were you planning to call that book about Spook Johnson's life?'

I flushed, embarrassed. 'My working title was *The Legend of Spook Johnson*.'

'Was that Johnson's idea?'

I nodded.

'I thought so! Then maybe you should begin a new book. We'll call it *The Legend of Spook Ward*.'

I studied his face. There wasn't even a flicker of humour in it. Was he serious? Were all spooks such vain sinners?

I was also alarmed to hear of this further delay in our mission. Nearly five days would have passed since Johnson was captured, before he had any hope of rescue. I was both hungry and exhausted, so I couldn't deny that the thought of a hot supper and a night in an inn seemed like heaven. But I felt riddled with guilt – what would this mean for Spook Johnson's chances of survival? I wondered fearfully.

The supper was good – a delicious venison stew – and we ate it alone at a table facing a roaring log fire. We were the only people in the dining room, which had almost been full when we'd first walked in. Within five minutes it had emptied.

Mr Ward didn't seem surprised. 'Being a spook is a lonely job,' he remarked. 'People keep their distance.'

'In Salford they certainly keep their distance from Spook Johnson,' I told him, 'but that's because they're afraid of him . . .'

'They're afraid of me too, but for different reasons. They don't like the work I do, even though it sometimes saves their lives. They think spooks are too close to the dark – that there must surely be unseen abominations following at our heels.'

'Are there?' I asked.

'Probably!' Mr Ward said, his expression deadly serious. 'The more the merrier!'

I stared at him. Did he welcome creatures from Hell so that he could make more money dealing with them?

'Don't be so serious, Brother Beowulf,' he said with a grin. 'You look like you've got the weight of the whole world on your shoulders. I was just teasing you, that's all. Nothing's following us, not even the Malkin clan's witch assassin. She's given up and gone back to Pendle to count her collection of thumb-bones.'

I smiled, relieved, and then a question popped into my head. 'There were names written on the wall of the bedroom I slept in at your house. I could tell they were past apprentices because Spook Johnson's name was there. But there was a girl's name there too – Jenny . . .'

The colour drained from Mr Ward's face. At first I thought he was angry with me. Then he gave a big sigh, and I realized he was simply sad. 'Jenny was my first and my only apprentice. Usually, a spook's apprentice has to be a seventh son of a seventh son. But Jenny was the seventh daughter of a seventh daughter. She was unique. But she died . . . She was killed by a water witch while we were travelling together . . .'

'I'm sorry,' I said lamely, wishing I'd never brought the matter up.

'It happens and I have to get used to it.' Ward shrugged, though I could tell he cared deeply. 'For all I joke about it, this is a very dangerous job. My own master, John

Gregory, trained over thirty apprentices in his long career fighting the dark. About a third of them died while learning the job.'

There was a long silence and I couldn't think of anything to say that might fill it. Why hadn't I kept my big mouth shut?

Mr Ward pushed his empty plate away. 'Noisy, aren't they?' he asked, nodding towards the bar, and the hubbub of voices and bursts of raucous laughter. Then somebody started to sing. A lone, tuneless male voice, but others quickly joined in and made it more melodious – and very loud.

'You take the room at the top of the stairs,' he said, rising from the table. 'Should be easier to sleep up there. I'll take the room directly above the bar.'

'You need your sleep too. What about tomorrow?' I asked.

'Oh, don't you worry about me, Brother Beowulf. I can sleep through anything. But I always wake up immediately when the situation demands it.'

'What sort of situation?' I wondered.

'Probably some slimy abomination from the dark slithering under the door of my room. That should do it. I think I'd wake up then!'

He gave me a big grin, and I found myself smiling back.

I was astonished to have a room all to myself. I thought again that spooks must be very well paid indeed for Mr Ward to afford two rooms. Mine was big, with plenty of space around the bed. There was even a table and a chair opposite the small window. On the table was a candle, a basin and a large jug of water.

Despite the chill in the room, I poured water from the jug into a basin and washed the grime from my shivering body. As Brother Halsall had taught us, cleanliness was next to godliness. Then I knelt down beside the bed and said a quick prayer to St Giles, asking him to keep away my night terrors. I might have decided not to be a monk any more, but that didn't mean I didn't have *some* faith.

Sometimes, just after I'd prayed to him, I saw St Giles out of the corner of my eye. He took the form of a stooped old man with a white beard and an exceptionally large, bulbous nose. When that happened, I usually had a quiet and peaceful night. This time, however, he didn't put in an appearance. Not a good sign.

I knew that the holy dead were out there somewhere, and sometimes a saint listened and helped. At other times they ignored me.

I got to my feet again and peered out of the window. I couldn't see much. There was a damp flagged yard below, and bedraggled trees in the distance. The clouds had cleared and a full moon was rising above them.

I'd never felt so tired in my life, and no sooner had my head touched the pillow than I fell asleep.

I woke up again just as quickly. Someone was talking to me, and the voice turned my heart to stone. I tried to close my ears to it. Why couldn't the dead just leave me alone?

I didn't open my eyes, but the voice seemed to be coming from the chair opposite the window.

'Help me! Help me!' called a deep masculine voice. *'The pain is terrible. It never ends!'*

Still I didn't open my eyes. Maybe it would go away, I thought, though mostly they persisted until I responded.

'Go away!' I cried. 'Leave me in peace.'

My heart began to pound. I knew it would be something horrible that I didn't want to see. The voice was definitely coming from the chair. The ghost was probably sitting in it.

I had to open my eyes to see it. Still I resisted.

'Help me! Help me, you ignoramus! Have you no pity? A monk should know better!' cried the voice, an edge of anger to its tone. Then it groaned in pain.

The word 'ignoramus' stung me. Brother Halsall had frequently called me an ignoramus during the first miserable weeks of my training when I was struggling to adjust to life at the abbey. I knew I wasn't ignorant or stupid, and I worked hard at my Latin to prove him wrong. He no longer called me that now, but I couldn't forget the loud braying voice that had brought smiles to the faces of all the other young monks – who had no doubt once received that same insult.

Ignoramus!

It was this insult which made me open my eyes in anger.

And I saw someone sitting in the chair.

Brother Halsall had told us that purgatory was a place where souls went. A place where they were cleansed by fiery pain so that they would be fit to enter into the Heavenly Kingdom.

I didn't believe in purgatory, but I did believe in Hell. I'd been given proof that it existed. Also I knew that there was pain after death. The pain suffered by these souls was usually the result of the horrible way in which they had died. They suffered it over and over again. Unless – sometimes – I could help them.

This one was bound with chains and it looked as if his throat had been cut from ear to ear – though I didn't inspect it too closely.

I knelt facing the poor tormented spirit and began to pray aloud. I was shivering with fear and revulsion, but I had to try. I always begin with the opening to Psalm 130, the *De Profundis*. I've tried others, but this seems to be the most effective prayer in such situations.

Someone or something usually answers.

'*Out of the depths I cry to thee, O Lord. Lord, hear my voice! Let Thine ears be attentive to the voice of my supplication.*'

There was no change. The wails of torment continued to increase – the soul was truly desperate, so I moved on to a significant line later in the prayer; one that usually worked.

'Eternal rest give to them, O Lord!'

There was still no change. There was only one thing left for me to do: I leaned forward and began to beat my forehead rhythmically against the floorboards. Sometimes inflicting pain upon myself seemed to help these souls. Perhaps my pain lessened theirs and allowed them to move on, I thought – though I couldn't be sure.

Each time my head made painful contact with the floor I cried out, 'Help him!'

And after a few minutes there was a sudden transformation. The wails ended abruptly and the soul gasped in surprise. I glanced up and saw that the spirit was shining brightly. The pain and horror on his face had been replaced by an expression of ecstatic joy.

The image slowly faded and I knew that I had been successful. He'd gone.

But now my whole body began to tremble in fear, for this was just the beginning of the nightmare.

I said that my nightmares had got worse while I was at the abbey, but that was really only half the story. For while I was learning to be a monk, I'd been visited by a demon. These visitations had been happening for almost ten months now – and they were terrible.

Usually it came to me during the night, immediately after I'd dealt with a poor suffering spirit.

The demon was proof that there was a Hell because he always knew what I had done.

I had saved a soul from Hell.

And there was a price to be paid.

The room became very cold and dark, and I looked up at the ceiling, towards the source of my increasing terror. My palms were sweating and my heart thumped erratically. Above me I saw that faint, sickly yellow light. Against this there was a moving pattern of darkness. At first it resembled the flickering shadows cast upon the ground by moonlight passing through the branches of a bare winter tree, its branches writhing under the force of a gale.

Then there came a change: the shadows resolved themselves into a vaguely human shape. It was a figure made of sticks, the image of the demon that always paid me a visit after I'd interceded for a soul. It had that strange body but its head lacked a face.

'Get behind me, demon! Leave me now!' I cried, knowing that my words were wasted.

The demon laughed; it was a harsh, mirthless sound, a mockery of my feeble command.

'That be no way to treat a friend,' it said, the voice deep and hoarse. *'You did well, boy, in releasing another poor suffering*

soul. I come only to reward you. That's the purpose of my visit. You should save such harsh words for an enemy and greet me warmly. I am your friend!'

'Don't mock me! You're no friend of mine!' I spat, knowing that I would be punished whatever happened.

I waited for the inevitable pain to enter my body; the agony that would throw me to the floor in convulsions, my back arching so severely that I feared my spine would snap.

Instead the demon gave me a vision, a glimpse of the near future . . .

I was walking across a high meadow with Mr Ward. Ahead of us were two men on horseback: the older man looked like a country squire; the younger one was dressed in the red uniform of a captain in the County military. A third man was on foot; he looked belligerent, burly and had a broken nose.

They intercepted us – forced us to halt.

There was a confrontation, a fight, and I saw Mr Ward collapse with a blade buried in his stomach.

There was a lot of blood.

As the Spook died in agony, I stood vomiting on the grass.

5

Lucky for Him

'Now you know what could happen, you can change that, can't you?' the faceless demon said. *'You'll find a way. That's my gift to you.'*

I simply looked up at it. The demon was leaving, and I could only be grateful.

The stick man on the ceiling was no longer writhing and twitching. It was as if the unseen wind that animated it was no more. It began to fade, and as it did so I fell unconscious.

When I awoke, I was stiff and cold because I'd been lying on the floor all night. The first dawn light was shining through the window.

I saw that I'd been sick on the floor – sufficient to make the room smell unpleasant. I opened the window wide and, after cleaning up the mess, washed myself thoroughly.

I dressed quickly and went downstairs. Mr Ward was already at the breakfast table, nibbling on a single piece of toast. He looked up and smiled.

'I always take a light breakfast when I'm about to face the dark,' he told me, 'but you go ahead and eat what you want. You'll need all your strength.'

Being sick in the night hadn't harmed my appetite. I was ravenous. So, needing no further encouragement, I ordered bacon, eggs and tomatoes. It was delicious.

Mr Ward watched me carefully as I ate. 'Sleep well?' he asked.

I nodded and he shrugged.

'It's just that you look pale – you've got dark circles under your eyes,' he went on. 'There's a bruise on your forehead too . . .'

'I stumbled in the dark and banged my head on the wall,' I lied. I was ashamed, but I hadn't told anyone about my so-called nightmares. I'd left that bit out of my story because I was afraid that the Spook would stop trusting me if he knew about them.

He nodded, but I could tell that he wasn't entirely convinced by my reply.

The moment I'd finished eating, we set off. After about twenty minutes' brisk walking we were climbing a slope that led up into a high meadow. It was a fine day – the sky was a brilliant blue without even one fluffy white cloud in sight, the sun was shining and the birds were singing.

Then I looked at the skyline, noted the pattern made by the trees and shivered with apprehension as I realized where we were. It was the place I'd been shown by the demon.

'Well, tell me about the witch – how did you approach her lair?' Mr Ward asked me. 'What exactly happened? How did an experienced hunter of witches like Spook Johnson fall into her trap?'

Before I could answer he shaded his eyes against the morning sun and gazed into the distance. Three men were approaching – two on horseback and one on foot. They were making directly for us.

It was exactly as it had happened in my vision. I began to tremble.

The men halted, barring our way.

'Turn back immediately!' commanded the elder of the two mounted men. 'I am Squire Anderton. This is *my* property and *you* are trespassing.'

The younger man, who was wearing the red jacket of a cavalry captain, smirked, radiating malevolence.

For the first time since I'd met him, I saw Mr Ward's face cloud with real anger. It was quite different to the emotion he'd shown when I'd tried to hurry him away from Chipenden. He looked up at the squire and scowled.

'I'm on urgent business, and unless I reach my destination very soon, lives may be lost,' he said, holding the rider's gaze. 'I can't afford to add an hour to my journey by going round the border of your land. Therefore I'll put it to you plainly: I mean to cross it.'

'In that case, be prepared to suffer the consequences!' cried the squire, nodding down at the man on foot, who was clearly his gamekeeper. 'Martin, teach this arrogant, ill-mannered oaf a lesson that he won't forget for the rest of his miserable days.'

The burly man had a heavy club tucked into his belt. He seized it eagerly and started to grin before tapping it rhythmically into the palm of his hand. The broken nose and aggressive stance suggested that he liked to brawl. He advanced upon Mr Ward, enjoyment dancing across his features; he looked like someone who delighted in inflicting pain upon others.

He balanced on the balls of his feet, then feinted, pretending to aim for Mr Ward's head – but the Spook didn't even blink. He just stood there silently, watching the man carefully, his staff held at an angle of forty-five degrees across his body.

Then Martin went on the attack for real, swinging the club with speed and skill, and Mr Ward began a slow retreat, sometimes nimbly avoiding the blows, occasionally blocking the club with his staff.

Martin's face reddened with fury as, thwarted again and again, he increased the pace of his attack. The sounds of thwacks and cracks of wood against wood rose to a crescendo.

When the Spook finally launched his own counterattack, it was so fast that I could hardly credit it, even though I'd already seen it in my vision.

With the end of his staff, he rapped Martin across the wrist to send the club spinning out of his hand into the long grass. When the gamekeeper went after it, the Spook used the base of his staff to prod him in the stomach and drive the air from his lungs. The man gasped and collapsed onto his knees.

Mr Ward laid his staff and bag down on the ground, then walked across to Martin, holding out a hand to help him to his feet.

'No hard feelings,' he said. 'I know you were only doing what you were told.'

All was exactly as I'd seen it in the vision. Martin bowed his head and groaned, apparently in pain and incapacitated. He put his right hand to his stomach as if about to rub it. Then, quickly and slyly, his hand continued down towards the hidden dagger.

'His boot!' I shouted. 'He's got a knife in his boot!'

Responding to my warning, Mr Ward immediately stepped aside, just avoiding the blade that arced upwards towards his stomach. Still it wasn't over. Martin lurched to his feet and went after him. The Spook's staff still lay out of reach on the ground where he'd placed it.

He took three rapid paces backwards, then halted so suddenly that Martin almost ran into him. His fist connected hard with the gamekeeper's chin, and there was the sound of knuckles crunching against jawbone. The man fell like a sack of potatoes, unconscious before he hit the ground.

Mr Ward strode past him, picked up his bag and staff, then gestured for me to follow.

However, the two horsemen were still glaring down at him.

'Let me deal with him, Father,' the young captain pleaded, but Squire Anderton shook his head.

'No, let it be,' he replied curtly. 'It's not seemly to brawl with a commoner.'

The captain flushed so deeply that his neck almost matched his jacket, and called angrily after us.

'If you were a gentleman, I'd fight you, sword against sword!'

Mr Ward turned to me and gave me another of his wolfish grins. 'I think it's lucky for him that I'm not a gentleman then!' he said cryptically.

Was he being serious? What chance would an untrained spook have with a sword against a captain from the County cavalry? Then again, I thought, this man was full of surprises.

We walked on through the long meadow grass. Just as we reached the trees, I glanced back. The gamekeeper was on his feet and all three men were staring after us. Moments later they were hidden from view. I shuddered – that had been a very narrow escape. And how strange that the help had come from my demon.

The Spook glanced at me as we walked. 'Thanks for the warning, Brother Beowulf. But how did you know that he had a blade tucked into his boot?'

'I saw it flash in the sunlight,' I said. I reasoned that it wasn't *quite* a lie because in my vision sunlight had indeed glinted off the metal blade as it cut into the Spook's belly.

'Did you now?' he said. 'You must have exceptional eyesight then, because I saw nothing.' He looked hard at me again, but I avoided meeting his eye. 'However, I really do mean thank you – you probably saved my life.'

'I'm just grateful that I saw it in time, Mr Ward,' I told him.

'Let's stop being so formal. You can call me Tom. What shall I call you? Do you prefer your full title? Or do you have a nickname?' he asked.

I pondered this. 'When I first entered the abbey, the other monks used to mock my name. But of course they have their fun with all noviciates. At first they shortened my name to Brother Wulf, but in the end I was just Cub.'

'Very original,' Tom said wryly. 'Well, if you don't mind it, I'll just call you Wulf. It's got a certain ring to it. Is that all right with you?'

I nodded. What he called me wasn't important, but it was the first time anyone had been nice enough to ask me about my name.

'Well, Wulf, shall we continue with the rest of your story?' Tom suggested. 'I need to know how Spook Johnson fell into the hands of the witch. But before that I'd like to hear a little more about him. What was it like being in his employ? Did he treat you well?'

I shrugged. 'I've no real complaints. I ate well enough, and he usually left me to get on with my writing. But in the evenings he drank a lot of red wine, and then he stayed in bed almost until noon. If he ever had to get up early he was like a bear with a sore head. He growled a lot and swore. It was best to keep out of his way.'

'Did he get many requests for help?' Tom asked.

I shook my head. 'On the whole folks kept away from his house – they only visited when their need was extreme. And he often turned people away. He refused to deal with ghosts and boggarts, claiming that he was a witch specialist.'

'I see. And how many witches does he have in his pits?' Tom wanted to know.

'None are in pits – he doesn't have any. He keeps them in the cells beneath his house.'

'Hmm, that's certainly unusual. Who'll be feeding them, with both you and Johnson gone?' He sounded concerned, as if he cared what happened to those creatures of the dark. He was a very strange spook, no doubt about it.

'He pays an old man to attend to them while he's away. But why are witches kept prisoner like that for so long?' I asked. 'Locking them up in pits and cells seems almost worse than killing them.'

'Perhaps it is. But some spooks do kill witches. There was a spook called Bill Arkwright who I worked with for six months to toughen me up. He was a good spook, but he was mean and ruthless. He used to give each water witch a sentence depending on how many humans she'd murdered. It was one year in a pit if she'd killed an adult and two years if the victim was a child.'

'That doesn't seem like a very harsh sentence, considering what they'd done,' I said, frowning.

Tom Ward raised an eyebrow. 'Doesn't it? Well, after the sentence was served, Arkwright would drag the witch out of the pit and kill her. I don't do that. I follow in the footsteps of my old master, John Gregory. The witches I capture stay in pits indefinitely. They might have a lifetime of suffering, but it keeps the County safe, and that's what's important. And besides, most witches should never be freed. Some kill for blood or bones to use in their magic, and some even specialize in slaying children.'

'I see . . . What was your master like?' I asked.

Tom paused for a few moments before he answered. I got the feeling that he was thinking carefully before he shaped his thoughts into words.

'He was without doubt the best spook who ever served the County, and a truly good and honest man. Even at an advanced age, he was fit and fearless, and his sense of duty was incredibly strong. He was more than willing to give his life if necessary. He's buried in the garden at Chipenden. I miss him. Very much.'

We walked on in silence. It was clear that Tom Ward had loved and respected his master, but there were things I still found hard to stomach. I could see that the people of the County had to be kept safe, but the whole business of dealing with witches seemed nasty and cruel to me. They were still human after all. It was even worse if what Spook Johnson had been accused of was true: if some of his prisoners were actually innocent of witchcraft.

Almost as if he'd read my mind, Tom said, 'You said we have to go through Salford to reach the witch's lair, so we'll check on Johnson's house on our way through. I want to take a look at those prisoners. How many did you say there were?'

'Eight at the moment. But don't you think it's best to press on and try to save Johnson? It's been days and days since he was captured!' I exclaimed.

Tom Ward shook his head. 'There are two possible scenarios. The first and most likely is that Spook Johnson's already dead. The second is that the witch is playing with him, taking her time before killing him. A quick call at the house isn't going to make much difference. Anyway, he was trained by John Gregory and, despite what looks like some failings along the way, Johnson has survived for years practising a dangerous trade. I'd like to know how the witch got the better of him. And while you tell me, I'll sort this out,' he said, sitting down on a tree stump and pulling off his right boot.

'The lace has snapped,' he said with a grin as I looked on, puzzled. 'That's what comes of walking around in the damp County . . .'

Tom rummaged around in his bag and pulled out a small ball of white string. While he replaced the lace, I told him what had happened.

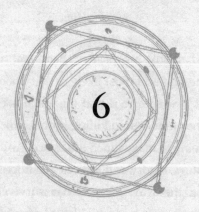

6

THE STALKING HORSE

The day had begun like any other. The previous evening, Spook Johnson had drunk two bottles of red wine and a large jug of ale, and consequently he'd slept well into the afternoon. I was writing at the kitchen table and I could hear him snoring upstairs. The whole house seemed to be vibrating to the rhythm.

Suddenly there was a loud knocking at the back door. I was about to respond when I heard Johnson's boots thumping down the stairs. There was a muffled conversation, and after about five minutes I heard the door slam and saw Johnson burst into the room, belly first.

'Get yourself ready, boy!' he shouted in his big booming voice. 'There's a witch to deal with, and not far from here. I'll have her safely locked up in a cell by midnight, but it's not good to work on an empty stomach. Get me some breakfast – five big pork sausages, greasy and hot, just as I like 'em!'

The Spook seemed to look upon me as his skivvy, giving me what he termed 'secondary duties'. It wasn't right, but I didn't actually mind cooking, and it was easier to do as I was told. I went into the kitchen and started to fry his sausages. Moments later he came in, sat down at the table, rolled up his sleeves and started to butter thick slices of bread. I served his late breakfast, then prepared to leave him to it.

However, he gestured towards the chair opposite him. 'Sit!'

I sat down and watched him eating. It wasn't a pretty sight. His mouth was big, but not large enough to keep up with the steady supply of greasy sausage that he was shovelling into it.

'I've recounted some of my recent dealings with witches, but I've never told you about the first one – the first witch I ever encountered.'

'Shall I go and get a pen and some paper?' I asked.

Johnson shook his head. 'No time for that – you can write it up tonight after we've attended to today's little problem. It's well worth including in the book though. It happened when I was an apprentice to old John Gregory. I'd been captured by a witch . . .'

He leaned towards me across the table and his voice became a whisper.

'She had really powerful magic. She turned me into a pig!'

His cheeks were red and bloated as he chewed. He couldn't have looked more like a pig right then if he'd tried. One part of me wanted to laugh, but the other was terrified that he'd glimpse the amusement in my eyes.

'But when the going gets tough, the tough get going!' he boasted. 'I sorted out that witch, but I didn't put her into one of Old Gregory's pits. I killed her familiar, then stabbed her right through the heart.'

He swallowed the last piece of sausage, wiped his greasy lips with the back of his hand, then lurched to his feet. He was a big man, and when I stood up I was still half a head short of his wide shoulders.

'Today you'll be able to study my classic procedure – the method I've refined for dealing with many witches. Note it well and record every detail. Right! Let's get on with it!'

Moments later he'd locked the door behind us and we were walking south down Salford's main street. Johnson was carrying his big staff and I was carrying his bag – another of the 'secondary duties' he'd assigned to me. Though my prime function was to gather material and write his book for him, these other duties seemed to take up a lot of my time. In addition to the cooking, I was expected to clean the house and feed his captive witches. When we were away, old Henry Miller did that job, and now Johnson sent me on ahead to rap on his door.

The stooped old man shuffled to open the door and spat at my feet in welcome. His eyes stared at a space somewhere near my left boot. He had a tuft of white hair above each ear, and his shiny bald head was covered in freckles and blotches.

'We're off on a job,' I told him, 'but we should be back tonight. Spook Johnson wants the witches fed before dark. They've had nothing since yesterday – they'll be hungry.'

Without meeting my eye, Old Henry slammed the door in my face. I knew he would do as he was told – he was too scared of Johnson to do otherwise.

We hadn't even reached the end of the main street before trouble caught up with us. I saw it coming.

There were three men waiting for us at the corner. One of them was Mr Chichester, the husband of one of the women Johnson had locked up. Most weeks, despite risking the wrath of the Spook, he came and knocked on the door and pleaded for his wife to be released. The two strangers accompanying him were big and burly – and they looked menacing.

One other thing made me wary. It was a Saturday afternoon – usually the main street was busy with people shopping – yet now there wasn't a soul in sight. The grocer, whose door was always open, especially in summer, had closed it. Where on earth was everyone?

As we drew alongside the men, one of them beckoned to us.

'Hey, Spook! We want a word with you.'

Johnson halted and turned to him. His face looked impassive and calm; however, there was a slight twitch at the corner of his left eye. You had to be really close to see it, but I knew what it meant. He was angry at being accosted, and ready to explode.

Taking slow, steady steps, he walked towards the three men. I followed at his heels, but not too closely. It was always best to give him plenty of room.

'We're going to take a little walk, fat man,' one of the thugs told him. 'And you're going to release Mr Chichester's wife.'

Johnson nodded at the man as if he was going to comply, then held his staff out behind him. I ran forward, grabbed it, and got well clear again. I was unable to see his face, but I knew that his left eye would be twitching violently. I saw the expressions on the faces of the two thugs change, and one slipped a hand into his pocket.

Johnson moved so quickly that, if you had blinked, you'd have missed it. He reached forward and grabbed each man by the scruff of the neck, then lifted them off their feet and banged their heads together with a dull, sickening crunch.

Then he simply threw them away. It was a long way too – two big arcs before they hit the cobbled street. One didn't get up, but the other staggered to his feet and moved towards Spook Johnson clutching a long-bladed knife.

Seconds later there was a snap like a twig breaking, and the man screamed, dropped the knife and fell to his knees nursing his wrist. It was broken, bent like a banana.

I looked on pityingly. He really shouldn't have called Johnson fat. He's sensitive about his belly: it grows and shrinks according to how many sausages he's eaten and how much ale and wine he's drunk. The truth is that most of him is muscle. He's hard and dangerous – certainly not a man to insult. The would-be attacker was lucky this had happened on the main street of Salford. Otherwise he could have ended up in a shallow unmarked grave.

'As for you,' Johnson said, glaring at Chichester, 'this is the only warning I'll ever give you. If you ever try something like this again, I'll break your scrawny neck. Understand?'

The man lowered his eyes to the ground, then looked up at the Spook, his face twisted in distress.

'I'm sorry, Mr Johnson, but you've made a mistake. My wife, Jenny – she isn't a witch. She wouldn't harm a fly!'

'Maybe that's because flies are her familiars,' Johnson retorted, his voice heavy with sarcasm. 'There are twice as many of 'em buzzing around her cell as in all the others put together.'

'Our children are suffering so,' Chichester continued. 'The youngest is only eight months old and she really misses her mam. She cries herself to sleep every night. It's heart-breaking.'

'That's enough!' Johnson said angrily. 'Your wife's cell is slopped out every two days and she's fed regularly. Some spooks keep their captive witches in pits, but mine are kept in humane conditions. You should be grateful.'

With that, he turned away from the man, glared at me until I handed back his staff, then strode off southwards at a rapid rate.

Once we were clear of the town, he beckoned me forward to walk alongside him.

'I'm going to tell you a little more of what we're about to face,' he said. 'The witch we're after is an incomer, which makes things more difficult. County witches come under three main classifications. Firstly, there are those dedicated to blood magic. They drink human blood – especially that of plump children – and that's how they get their magical power. Then there are bone witches, who usually slice off their victim's thumbs. Some wear those bones on necklaces around their necks. When the need takes 'em, they stroke the bones and draw on their magical power.'

Johnson fell silent for a while. I knew he was thinking about something from his past. He seemed to have forgotten all about me. I was just about to drop back and let him take the lead when he suddenly grabbed my shoulder and continued speaking as if he'd never stopped.

'Witches who use familiar magic can be the most dangerous of all because it's not always easy to work out what their familiar is. Most use cats, dogs, toads, rats, mice or crows, but sometimes the creatures they use don't belong in this world – they're entities straight from the dark, and they can come in all sorts of shapes and sizes. But whatever hideous form they take, they're the eyes, ears, hands and sometimes the teeth and claws of their mistress, and will do anything in exchange for being allowed to suck her blood.'

I knew most of what Spook Johnson was telling me – I'd peeked into his library – but I allowed him to drone on without interruption. He liked the sound of his own voice and it would put him in a good humour.

'Because this witch is an incomer,' he continued, 'because she comes from outside the County, we've no record or history of what she's capable of. She could be one of those three types or something totally new. So, boy, we're stepping into the unknown. She's taken up residence in an abandoned village and is starting to prey on nearby farms. Folk have gone missing. The lad who knocked on our door was on the road with his family. They were prepared to leave behind most of their possessions and take their chances elsewhere. He said she'd killed people. She's only been there a week, but she's already got the local farmers scared out of their wits. We need to proceed with caution, but I still hope to have her safely locked up by midnight. And now for your role in all this. You're going down there alone – you'll be my stalking horse . . .'

That got my attention. My blood froze as I listened to him in astonishment. I was his scribe, not his apprentice! It wasn't my job to go into danger alone. I was terribly afraid. I was a noviciate monk and the witch would see me as a threat to be eliminated as quickly as possible. While she moved against me, Johnson would be waiting in the background unseen, ready to deal with her. He was using me as a decoy to cover his own attack. I could be killed or, worse, I might fall into the clutches of a practitioner of the dark arts. My very soul might be in jeopardy.

'It's the best way to deal with a witch of unknown powers,' he explained. 'I've used it with great success in the past. Usually I'd send an apprentice down to do the job, but unfortunately I don't have one at the moment. So you'll have to do instead.'

I wondered if any of his apprentices had survived such a dangerous task.

'Did you have any apprentices that became spooks?' I asked, not really wanting to know the answer.

Johnson shook his head. 'I've been unlucky with my apprentices – none of them were any good. The last one ran away. No guts. You have to be brave to do this job. But don't worry – I'll be watching you every step of the way. The first sign of danger and I'll be there!'

That didn't fill me with confidence.

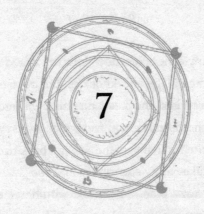

7

SOMETHING WRONG

We reached the brow of a hill and there, below us in the twilight gloom, was the abandoned village. It was small – almost a hamlet. But just as some people call a town a city if it's got a cathedral, others consider a hamlet to be a village if it has even the meanest of churches.

This church was small and built of local stone, but lacked a spire or a tower. However, it had a big, impressive solid-oak door which had a smaller one set within it. Apart from this, the village consisted of a shop and a single cobbled street with maybe a couple of dozen houses, most of them with broken windows and doors hanging off their hinges. Close by stood a farmhouse, complete with barn. There was fenced land too, but no animals to be seen.

It looked peaceful enough, but the witch would be in residence somewhere in that street.

'Don't look so nervous, boy,' Johnson urged me. 'Just go down into the village and knock on the door of that shop. Pretend you're lost and need directions. There's a church there. That should make you feel better. When you find out where the witch is living, come straight back up the hill and we'll try to take her by surprise.'

It was a crazy plan. Surely she would see me coming! According to the books in Johnson's library, some witches could sniff out danger long before it arrived. Perhaps she already knew that a spook was in the vicinity. I'd be like a fly blundering into a spider's web.

But Johnson merely patted me on the shoulder and sat with his staff across his knees. 'Leave the bag with me. Off you go!'

I put his heavy bag next to him and set off down the hill.

I was facing south and the village street ran from east to west below me. Before I reached the road, I veered off into a small wood that almost reached the back gardens of the nearest row of houses. That leafy canopy would hide me from the gaze of anybody watching from below. I walked slowly, trying to keep my approach as silent as possible, doing my best to avoid stepping on any twigs. It was unnaturally quiet among the trees. There was no birdsong – not even a buzz of insects.

My heart was beating rapidly as I left the cover of the trees and crossed a grassy patch between two cottages to emerge onto the cobbled street.

Something Wrong

I headed directly towards the shop, and saw a sign above the window stating the name of the owner:

BATLEY'S GENERAL STORE

I tried the door, and the handle turned easily. I eased it open and, very cautiously, stepped inside. I closed it behind me and stood with my back against it, waiting for my heart rate to slow down and my eyes to adjust to the gloom.

There was something wrong here, I thought. The village was clearly abandoned but this shop was full to the rafters with goods. Stacked on the floor were sacks of vegetables – potatoes, carrots, swedes, turnips and onions – and the shelves were stocked with packets and bags holding all manner of things, from tea and sugar to herbs and medicines. As well as pots and pans, there were slabs of salted meat hanging from hooks, and crates of ale and wine stood in the corner.

But what was the point when there were no customers? I wondered. Could the shopkeeper possibly still be living here?

A shiver ran down my spine, and suddenly I realized that I wasn't alone in the room. A bright flash of red drew my gaze. A child stood by the counter looking up at me – a little girl with bright red hair; its glow dispelled the gloom of the shop's interior. She was very young, no more than three or four, but there was something intense in the gaze from her large green eyes that suggested a maturity far beyond her years.

'Is your mam or your dad around?' I said, giving her my friendliest smile.

'Mr Batley had a heget!' she declared.

'What's a heget?' I asked.

She looked annoyed, then pointed at her own head and frowned. 'The heget was hurting Mr Batley's head but the pain soon passed. He feels much happier now,' she said.

I suddenly realized what she meant. 'You mean he had a headache?'

'Yes, he had a bad heget but he didn't want it. What do *you* want, priest? Are you looking for the witch?'

I was surprised by the almost rude way she'd addressed me as 'priest'. Although she looked like a child, and apart from that one odd lapse in vocabulary – calling a headache a 'heget' – I felt again that there was something uncannily adult about her; there was a challenge in her gaze.

'Yes, I'm looking for the witch,' I told her. 'Do you happen to know where she is?'

'Of course I do. I'll show you, if you like . . .'

Before I could reply, she seized me by the hand, opened the shop door and pulled me out onto the street. Her hand felt very cold. I looked up at the sky, which was lit by a strange red glow; dark clouds were blustering in from the west. In the distance I heard a faint rumble of thunder. It is fair to say I was afraid.

'This way,' the child said. 'It isn't far.'

When I hesitated, she tugged me along fiercely. She halted near the door of the fifth cottage from the shop and pointed at the window.

'She's asleep. There's no danger. Why don't you peep through the window?' she suggested, releasing my hand.

I approached the window cautiously. What if the witch saw me peering in at her? I thought fearfully. However, I was emboldened by the sound that reached my ears. The witch was asleep and was snoring almost as loudly as Spook Johnson did.

She was sprawled in a rocking chair, her mouth wide open and her eyes closed. She was dressed in black and there was a broomstick leaning against her chair. I could see that there was something very strange about her face, but in the gloom I couldn't see clearly enough to work out what. I decided it was something to worry about later – I had to bring Johnson to the cottage while she was still asleep.

'Go and get your master, priest!' the little girl told me. 'And be quick about it before she wakes. The witch is dangerous. She ate three plump babies yesterday!'

There was evident glee in her voice when she told me about the babies. I stared at her in horror. Surely she couldn't be serious! The idea was too horrible to even joke about. I saw that the corners of her mouth were turned up, ready to break into a smile. And how, I wondered, did she know that Spook Johnson was waiting up the hill?

'Go home,' I told her crossly. Then I turned my back on her, raced across the street and walked up into the trees. I stayed in their shadow until I reached Spook Johnson; I saw him standing at the top of the hill so I beckoned to him.

His response was to wave back furiously, insisting that I came up to him. I sighed. No doubt he wanted me to carry his bag. I waved again, and this time he strode down towards me carrying his bag and staff, his face red with anger.

'Next time I ask you to come, you'd better come running!' he warned.

'I'm sorry, but it was faster for you to come down to me. The witch is asleep. You can take her by surprise!' I told him.

'A man of my ability and experience doesn't need to take a witch by surprise!' he snapped, and started rummaging about in his bag. He pulled out his silver chain and wrapped it around his left wrist and forearm. Then he thrust the bag at me.

Carrying his staff and chain, he set off down the hill at a furious pace, not bothering to keep within the cover of the trees. By now the clouds overhead were really thick and the first heavy drops of rain were falling. I stumbled along behind him.

'Where is she?' Johnson called back over his shoulder when we reached the village.

'Fifth cottage on the left after the shop,' I said.

He headed directly towards it, but he was too late. The witch must have heard his big boots on the cobbles, or his shout.

She had come out to meet him.

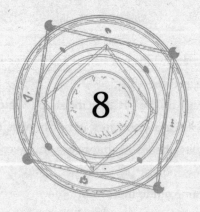

8

THE STORYBOOK WITCH

The witch quickly looked right and left down the street as though looking for someone and, for the first time, I saw her face properly.

I'd already suspected it was oddly proportioned, but her profile was a shock all the same. From her forehead to her long chin it was concave, like a crescent moon. Her eyes were bulbous, her nose was huge, and there was a big wart on the end of her chin. Her big hands had long sharp nails.

She stared at Spook Johnson and gave a loud cackle that was edged with insanity.

Suddenly I recognized her. I had seen that face before. She was straight out of the book I'd been given to copy early in my noviciate. A rich landowner was paying a lot of money into the abbey's coffers to have the copy made. It was to be a birthday present for his young daughter. It had illustrations, but someone else was reproducing those. I was just copying the text. The original book was literally falling to pieces.

The story told of an evil witch who was slain by a brave young prince. One particular illustration had caught my eye, for the witch had been drawn in an exaggerated manner.

I was now looking at the witch from that storybook, complete in every detail, from the concave face to the wart on her chin. She was nothing like the other witches I'd encountered while serving Spook Johnson. She seemed weird, unreal – like something out of a nightmare.

Then I remembered the broom that had been propped against her chair. In the story the witch had flown on that broomstick. Would she do so now? I wondered.

In the distance I saw a flash of lightning, and when it faded the street was almost in darkness, the storm clouds swirling overhead. Johnson and the witch just stood there, staring at each other. The crash of distant thunder seemed to be the signal for the witch to launch herself at her adversary. She shrieked and ran at him, hands outstretched, long talons ready to gouge out his eyes.

I thought Spook Johnson was about to suffer this fate, but at the last moment he stepped aside and the talons missed his face. He was surprisingly quick and nimble for such a big man.

As the witch lost her balance and fell to her knees, her hand scraped across the ground. Her long nails created a deep furrow, tearing up cobbles and even cutting one in two. If that had been Johnson's face, it would have been the end of him.

The witch was on her feet again in a second, and Johnson began to back away. Was he retreating? Was he afraid of the witch? Then, as he reached for his silver chain, I realized that he was just giving himself room. I'd already seen him cast his chain at a witch, and knew that he was very skilled.

He allowed his staff to fall onto the cobbles and concentrated on the throw. It was perfect. With a great swoop of his arm, he sent the chain into a spiral in mid-air above his target. It lassoed the witch, encircling her from head to knee, tightening as it bound her.

She fell full-length on the cobbles and flopped around like a freshly hooked salmon. She was oddly silent – but it didn't seem to bother Johnson, who simply picked her up and slung her over his shoulder.

Then, with a curt 'Bring my bag and staff!' in my direction, he set off back towards Salford.

When he reached his house he ordered me to make him a brew while he carried the witch down the steps to the cells.

I'd just placed his big mug of tea on the table when he reappeared, rubbing his hands.

'Sit down, boy!' he commanded. I did so and faced him across the table. He was grinning widely. When in a good mood, Johnson was almost pleasant to be with, and he was never happier than when he'd dealt with a witch.

'Well! What did you think of that?' he demanded.

'The witch never had a chance. You made a perfect cast with your chain,' I said, telling him exactly what he wanted to hear – though it was all perfectly true. 'I'll write it up in full before I go to bed.'

He beamed at me and blew on his tea before sipping it.

'But don't you think she's a strange-looking witch?' I asked him. 'She has a face like the horned moon.'

'I've seen hags that looked stranger than that!' he exclaimed. 'I once killed a witch with a face like a dog. She barked at me, but quickly started howling when I stuck her with my blade. You see all sorts of odd things in this game, boy.'

Then I remembered the little girl and I shivered. There was something wrong with her, I knew. Somehow I suspected that this encounter wasn't over yet.

'It's not for me to tell you your job, Mr Johnson, but I think there's something else in that village that might need attending to,' I said to him.

'Oh? What makes you think that?' he demanded with a frown, his happiness and bonhomie cooling more rapidly than his tea.

'I spoke to a little girl – it was she who showed me where the witch was to be found. There was something about her that I didn't like. She was creepy. I wonder if she's linked to the witch in some way. Maybe she's her daughter—'

'But why would she betray her own mother?' Spook Johnson scoffed.

'I don't know, but I think she lived in the shop: her father is probably Mr Batley, the shopkeeper. She said he was upstairs with a bad headache – but why were they there at all if the rest of the village was abandoned? There's something very strange about the whole thing. Perhaps we should go back and talk to him. Then maybe visit some of the nearby farms and tell people that, thanks to you, all is now safe.'

Until those last few words Johnson had looked ready to explode. He didn't like being told what to do. However, the last bit of praise calmed him down.

'You're right, boy. It wouldn't do any harm to let the locals know that I've saved their bacon. We'll take a stroll back there tomorrow. Now get on with your work. Give a detailed account of what happened, and don't forget to describe my bravery when that dangerous witch charged at me. I made the perfect capture, didn't I?'

'You certainly did,' I agreed. 'I'm looking forward to writing it all up. It'll make an exciting episode in your life story.'

That night Johnson sat in the kitchen drinking wine while I went up to my room to record the day's events.

I didn't mention the fact that he'd wasted the chance to take the witch by surprise, but described his confrontation with her in detail. Sometimes I had to exaggerate his actions in order to please him – although there was no need for that here. I wondered how long he'd had to practise in order to become so proficient with his silver chain.

Johnson was a big strong man, but witches could display incredible strength. I remembered how this witch's talons had sliced into the heavy stone cobbles. The Spook had faced her bravely: only his skill with the silver chain had stopped her from tearing his face off.

I'd almost finished my account when there was a loud knocking at the front door. Once he'd sat down and started to drink his wine, Johnson never usually answered the door. This was another of my jobs. Irritated at having been disturbed when I was so close to finishing my writing, I went downstairs in a bit of a temper.

There was a young woman at the door, wearing the long skirt and sheepskin cloak typical of a farmer's wife or daughter. As soon as I saw her, my anger dissipated and my heart softened. She had a pretty face but her eyes were red and swollen. She was in tears, hardly able to control her sobbing.

At last she took a deep breath and blurted out what had happened.

'I need the Spook to help me. I'm desperate. It killed my husband, and now my little son is trapped in the house! If I don't get help, it'll kill him too!'

'What killed your husband?' I asked gently, trying to find out what had happened.

'A boggart! It's been throwing small stones for weeks,' she explained. 'To begin with they just fell in the yard and in the fields – it was just a nuisance. Then they started falling on the roof during the night, keeping us awake. One night my husband couldn't stand it any longer. He opened the bedroom window and swore at the boggart. Then, today, he didn't come back for his lunch. I found him in the field. His head had been crushed by a boulder.'

The woman started crying again, and it was a while before I could get her to continue.

'How did your son come to be trapped in the house?' I asked her.

'I left him inside when I went out to the field. When I got back, both doors were jammed shut. I could hear my little boy crying inside. Please ask the Spook to help!' she cried.

I nodded and went to speak to Johnson. He'd told me often enough that he specialized in dealing with witches and didn't bother with other types of creature from the dark. Surely he'd make an exception in this case, I thought. After all, a child was in mortal danger.

'It's a woman whose husband has just been killed – her small son is trapped inside the house, crying for help. The creature has sealed both the doors,' I reported.

Johnson looked up at me with bloodshot eyes. He had been celebrating his success and had just started on his third bottle of wine.

'You said "creature" . . . You mean a witch?' he slurred, frowning.

I shook my head. 'She said it's a boggart – the type that throws stones. It's not far away. She lives in Colt Farm, a fifteen-minute walk from here,' I told him.

'Are you stupid, boy? Don't waste my time with stone-chuckers! Send the woman away. I only deal with witches!' Johnson retorted.

I rarely answered him back but I was angry. I couldn't stop thinking about the poor woman whose husband was dead; there was nobody else to help rescue her child.

'But why?' I cried angrily. 'Why just limit yourself to witches when people need help against other hellish creatures?'

The Spook stared up at me, but to my surprise he looked calm, his face strangely melancholic. 'When I was an apprentice,' he replied, 'I faced witches many times and grew to hate them. Forget boggarts, ghosts and other creatures. Witches are female and they're devious – they're the deadliest of all the creatures of the dark! I decided there and then that I'd be the best spook witch hunter who'd ever lived. And now that's what I am. I save all my strength for witches. That should be a spook's priority and I've made it mine.'

'But if you don't help, a child could die!' I exclaimed.

He didn't reply, and a moment later his shoulders slumped and he bowed forward until his forehead made gentle contact with the tabletop. Within moments he was snoring.

I went to the door to talk to the woman again. When I told her of my master's refusal to help, she sobbed loudly and tore her hair.

Despite my fear, her plight gave me no choice.

I accompanied her back to the farm, hoping that I might be able to help.

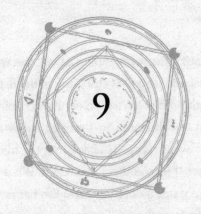

9

THE STONE-CHUCKER

We walked fast. The woman was still in tears, and I prayed silently. By now the sun had set and darkness covered the land.

We left a small wood and saw the farm ahead of us, silhouetted against the pale grey sky. I could hear the cries of the child. He kept calling out one shrill word over and over again:

'Mam! Mam! Mam!'

The farm was small – just a house, a yard and a barn that was hardly larger than a shed. There was a meadow containing a dozen sheep, and a milk cow tethered to a fence. As we approached, I heard small sounds all around us. At first I thought it had started to rain, but then I realized that small pebbles were falling through the air and swishing down onto the grass.

'The boggart's throwing stones at us!' the woman cried. 'My poor husband's body is still lying in the field. How will I manage without him? What on earth am I going to do?'

She began to sob again, so I moved closer and pointed back the way we'd come. 'Go back into the trees where it's safe,' I told her. 'I'll go and get your child. What's his name?'

'Bobby. His name's Bobby . . . and I'm Laura,' she added.

'Hide in the trees then. I'll go for Bobby.'

She nodded and headed back towards the small wood. When I reached the gate, I lifted the latch, eased it open a little and squeezed through. I was about halfway across the yard when the first big stone struck the ground to my left. It was big enough to knock me unconscious – or worse.

I knew a little about boggarts, thanks to peeping into Johnson's library to learn as many spooks' secrets as I could. The books in that library weren't just limited to witches. They covered the whole range of evil entities that spooks dealt with. I'd learned that although most stone-chucker boggarts were simply annoying, some could be dangerous killers.

And there was no doubt about this one. The poor farmer was dead and I could well be next.

Sensing a movement on the roof of the house, I glanced up and saw the boggart.

I knew that boggarts usually stayed invisible, though some took on the shapes of animals – cats, rats, dogs or even horses. However, I also knew that stone-chuckers resembled humans in shape and stood upright on two legs – though they had six arms. There was a sketch of one of them in a book I'd glanced through. The thing balancing on the apex of the roof showed it to be accurate.

I could just see it against the darkening sky. In each of its six hands was a missile – some were small stones, but some were huge. I moved closer to the door until I couldn't see the boggart any more. This meant that it couldn't see me either.

Not really expecting to be successful, I turned the handle of the front door. It opened inwards so I pushed as hard as I could. There had been nothing in the book about boggarts being able to lock doors, but this one didn't shift an inch. Somehow the house had been sealed.

How could I get it open before the boggart brained me? I wondered. Prayer was sometimes the answer, but it was important to use the correct words and find the right saint.

I searched my memory, skimming through a list of patron saints. One name winged its way into my head:

St Quentin, the patron saint of locksmiths.

I began to pray to him, begging for his help.

'St Quentin, I beg thee to open this door. It's been locked by a servant of Hell. Help me save that poor child!' I called out.

As I prayed, I kept up my pressure on the handle and leaned heavily against the door. It still didn't move. I repeated the prayer over and over again, finally shortening it until it was reduced to 'Please open the door! Please open the door!' – and with each repetition of 'please' I beat my forehead hard against the wood.

I could hear the rhythmical thumps, each blow increasing my pain, but I was also aware that the child was no longer calling out for his mam. I hoped he was all right.

At one point a rock bigger than my head came down, missing my left shoulder by inches to thud into the ground. My knees began to tremble. Had that one hit me I'd be dead, I thought. Until then I'd just been nervous, my concern for the trapped child overwhelming my fear. But now I was terribly afraid. The boggart must have moved to a point where it crouched directly above me. At any moment my head might be cracked open like an egg, my brains dashed from my fragile skull.

'Open the door! Open the door!' I continued, still beating my head against it.

Finally, when my head was throbbing with pain, St Quentin came to my aid.

What I saw was so faint as to be hardly visible, so grey and transparent that I could see right through it. Suddenly, over my left shoulder, a long hairy arm reached towards the door. It was holding a key, which it inserted into the lock and then twisted. Immediately the door yielded, and I fell through it onto my knees.

Muttering my thanks to the saint, I came to my feet and stumbled forward into the first of the dark rooms, calling out Bobby's name. A little dark-haired boy wearing a grey shirt stained with tears and snot emerged from another room and tottered towards me, clearly terrified. I picked him up quickly, then ran out, eager to get clear of the house before the boggart realized what was happening.

I was almost safe when a rock caught me a glancing blow on the temple. I staggered and almost fell, but even though my legs felt like jelly, fear drove me onwards. I could feel blood, wet and warm, running down the side of my face.

Then I'd reached the wood, safely out of range of the boggart's missiles. I handed the sobbing boy to his mother. She hugged him close, and murmured heartfelt thanks to me.

'Is there anywhere you can go for shelter?' I asked. 'Do any of your family live nearby?'

'My sister Anne is a good woman. She'll take us in,' Laura told me, crying with relief at being reunited with her son.

It was an hour's journey through the dark to the sister's house.

As Laura bathed my head over the kitchen sink, she told her sister about the boggart that had killed her husband and threatened the life of her little boy.

'The Spook refused to help, but this boy, his apprentice, came in his stead . . .' she said.

I felt like protesting that I wasn't Johnson's apprentice, but I was weary and my head hurt too much. I was struggling to speak.

'He was brave and he saved Bobby's life. Thank you!' she said, kissing me on the cheek. I felt myself blushing, but then she rubbed iodine into my wound, and it took all my self-control not to scream out in agony.

'What about Daniel's body?' Anne asked. 'Is it still lying in the field?'

That started Laura crying again.

'I'll try to sort something out tomorrow when it gets light,' I promised her.

However, despite my best intentions, I was unable to keep that promise.

It was a weary trudge back to Spook Johnson's house, and when I got there I was in for a shock.

Even before I went inside, I knew that something was wrong. The front door stood wide open and there were drops of blood on the step.

With trepidation I crossed the threshold. The chair where Johnson sat had been overturned and the empty bottles of wine lay smashed under the table. What pooled under the chair could have been red wine – but it wasn't. The air was tainted with the metallic odour of blood.

I went down to the cellar. The witches near the door were still in their cells, but they were agitated. They whined, rolled their eyes and hissed at me. I went further into the cellar, knowing full well what would confront me. And, indeed, the cell that had held the witch from the abandoned village was empty. In a display of incredible strength, the bars had been bent wide. She must have bided her time after Johnson released her from his silver chain, then broken out. I cursed his arrogance. She was clearly dangerous – how could he have been so stupid?

I went out into the street and followed the drops of blood far enough to see that the witch was carrying Spook Johnson away to her lair. At first I considered following her. Then I realized I could do nothing alone. I felt bad leaving Johnson in the witch's clutches, but what chance did I have against her?

I needed help.

As before, I had omitted certain things from the account I gave Tom Ward. I'd heard of a spook called Ward because Johnson had mentioned the name, calling him 'a young whippersnapper' among other derogatory terms. Still, he sounded like my best bet. The only problem was, I didn't know where to find him.

However, that night I awoke suddenly, sure that somebody had called my name. Even as I blinked away sleep, the stick figure with no face began to appear on the ceiling.

'Get behind me, demon! Leave me now!' I cried, filled with dread.

The demon took no notice, and I cringed both in fear and in anticipation of the pain it was sure to inflict. Sometimes it made my back arch so that I feared my spine might snap like a twig; sometimes my eyes and throat felt as if they were being pierced with hot needles.

'Please!' I shouted. 'Don't hurt me again. Leave me alone, I beg you.'

The demon laughed long and loud.

'I'm not here to inflict pain on your body. I think you need a little help, and I know where it is to be found.'

It chuckled and I flinched, assuming that it was tricking me and would strike out at any moment.

'Spook Ward lives in a village called Chipenden. It is in the north of the County, west of a big hill called the Long Ridge. If you start at dawn, it will take you almost two days to get there. But you might still be in time to save your master.'

The demon left me; I felt weak and I was sweating with fear.

But it was enough to send me to the house of Tom Ward.

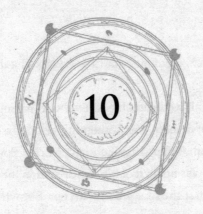

10

THE PICK OF THE BUNCH

Tom came to his feet and stamped his right boot hard on the ground a couple of times. 'That string should do for a while,' he said, before looking at me with a frown on his face.

'Listen – don't feel bad about leaving Johnson,' he continued. 'You did the right thing. And you were brave to rescue that child, Wulf. Not many people would have dared to do what you did. You could have been killed.'

I shook my head. 'I wasn't brave. I just did what had to be done. There was nobody else to help, so it had to be me,' I explained.

'But that's often the way of it,' Tom countered. 'That's a situation I've faced many times – it's exactly what I've told myself too. The first time was at the very beginning of my apprenticeship, when I was just a twelve-year-old boy. Being the only one there puts pressure on you to be brave. But you did have a choice. You could have walked away, and you didn't.'

'I'd never have been able to live with myself if I'd done that. Oh – and there was something else,' I said, suddenly remembering. 'After the witch had carried Spook Johnson away, there was no sign of his bag or staff in the house. I can only think that she took them with her. But why would she do that?' I asked.

Tom frowned. 'I don't know, Wulf,' he said. 'That's very unusual behaviour for a witch, and usually they're unable to touch a staff made of rowan wood.'

We fell silent for a few moments. We were approaching Salford now, and I could see buildings in the distance shrouded by low grey clouds and drizzle. The scene was dismal. Then Tom asked me something.

'When you prayed to get the door open, why did you bang your forehead against it?' he said curiously.

'Some monks use flagellation as a way to punish themselves – they whip themselves in the hope that it will somehow cleanse their souls of sin,' I explained, 'or they wear shirts made of coarse itchy cloth under their habits to make themselves uncomfortable. I would never do anything like that – I think it's senseless. But in extremis, when the situation is so dire that it warrants it, I've found that banging my head against something and hurting myself makes it more likely that my prayers will be answered.'

Tom didn't look convinced, but he gave me a friendly smile before suddenly frowning again. I glanced sideways and saw that he was deep in thought.

'Do they treat you badly at the abbey?' he asked. 'Is that why you want to leave?'

I shook my head, and then I told him something I'd never told anybody else before. 'It's because I've lost my faith,' I said. 'I no longer believe in God. What's the point of being a monk if you don't believe in God?'

Tom gave me a sympathetic smile. 'I'll wager you aren't the only monk who doesn't believe in God,' he told me. 'At least as a monk you eat regular meals, have a roof over your head and sometimes do some good. Copying books preserves and shares knowledge. And no doubt you help the poor. But explain one more thing to me, if you don't mind. If you don't believe in God, then why do you bother to pray?'

'Because it works,' I replied. 'The Church teaches us to use saints as intermediaries – they intercede for us and pass our prayers on to Him. We aren't actually supposed to pray directly to them. But I do the opposite. I don't pray to God, I pray to the saints. And sometimes they help me.'

'So you don't believe in God, but you do believe in the saints?' Tom chuckled, clearly amused by my logic. 'And did you really did see the arm of St Quentin unlocking that door? Are you sure you didn't imagine it?'

'It was very faint – but, no, it wasn't just my imagination. When the saints help me, they don't always make themselves visible like that, but their help is real enough,' I insisted.

Tom grinned wryly and I felt my face growing hot.

'And what about you?' I demanded angrily. 'You fight creatures from Hell. Do *you* believe in God?'

He looked thoughtful. 'That's a good question, Wulf, and the truth is that I'm not sure. John Gregory, my master, once said something that sums up the position I'm moving towards. He told me that once or twice he'd faced such extreme danger that he'd had little hope of survival. But then – right in that impossible moment – he felt as if he'd been helped by some unseen presence.'

'He thought that was God?' I said, astonished.

'That or maybe God's messenger.' Tom Ward shrugged. 'Well, Wulf, that's enough theology for today. Now for more practical matters. When you left Johnson's house, did you tell that old man to feed the captive witches?' he asked me.

'Of course I did,' I huffed. 'I knew I'd be away for some time. Even if they're witches, I wouldn't like them to die thanks to lack of water or food.'

'Right you are! In which case, lead me to Johnson's house and we'll take a look at them.'

*

Soon I was taking Johnson's front door key out of my pocket and letting us in.

Wasting no time, we went straight down to the cellar. It smelled terrible – of urine and worse. Even though the torch was still flickering on the wall and the witches had been fed, I don't think Old Henry had bothered to slop out the buckets for at least a couple of days.

Most of the witches were asleep when we entered, and the room echoed with the drone of their snores. Perhaps snoring was a disease they'd caught off Spook Johnson, I thought to myself. One or two were awake and they stared at Tom malevolently. One sniffed loudly three times. His cloak and staff would give him away, but I wondered if, even without the flickering light from the torch, they'd still be able to sense that he was a spook.

He walked along the cells, pausing at each one, then coming to a sudden halt at the cell from which the witch had escaped. He examined the bent bars carefully and shook his head.

'That shows incredible strength!' he exclaimed, but I felt the remark was addressed to himself rather than to me.

He moved on, only to halt again outside the final cell next to the wall. The woman inside was watching him carefully, but there was no hatred or anger on her face – just sadness.

'What's your name?' Tom asked her, his voice very soft.

'They call me Jenny,' she replied in a whisper.

He flinched, as if the name was a blow. He even took a small step backwards, and I wondered if he was thinking about the apprentice who'd died.

I went up to him. 'This is Mrs Chichester, the witch I told you about,' I told him. 'Her husband is always protesting her innocence and begging Spook Johnson to set her free. He's the one I told you about – he hired those thugs to accost Johnson in the High Street.'

Tom nodded, and then beckoned to Mrs Chichester. She left her bench and approached the bars tentatively.

'Mrs Chichester, would you mind if I held your left hand for a moment? There's something I need to know. Doing that will help me to make up my mind,' he asked her gently.

Without hesitating, the woman did so, and he grasped her hand for no more than a couple of seconds. Then he released it and smiled at her. 'I'm sorry that you've been imprisoned. It was a mistake and should never have happened. You'll be back with your family soon.'

She smiled at Tom and tried to speak, but no words came out, and tears ran down her cheeks.

Tom turned to face me. 'Let Mrs Chichester out and escort her home,' he said. 'She's no malevolent witch. She may use a little magic, but she's benign.'

'But what about Spook Johnson?' I protested. I was pleased that Mrs Chichester was being freed, but I could only imagine how angry Johnson would be. 'He'll go berserk when he finds out what we've done!'

'Leave Johnson to me,' Tom said. 'Now, once you've reunited Mrs Chichester with her husband, come straight back here and—' He halted mid-sentence and smiled sheepishly. 'I'm sorry, Wulf. I seem to be snapping orders at you as if you were my apprentice. I'd *like* you to do those things. It would help me a lot, but they're requests – not orders.'

I smiled back. 'Of course I don't mind. I'll be back as soon as I can.'

'Thank you, Wulf. One more thing – where does the old man live?' he asked me.

'Henry Miller? On the main street, number thirty-seven,' I replied. I wondered why he wanted to know, but instead I took the bunch of keys, unlocked the cell door and did as Tom had asked.

It was still drizzling outside. I walked beside Mrs Chichester in silence. I wanted to speak to her but didn't know where to begin. What could you say to a woman who'd been wrongly imprisoned for many months? I now saw the contrast between Tom Ward and Spook Johnson. They were both spooks, but they approached the job very differently. Johnson was bad-tempered, judgemental and impulsive. Ward was quiet, thoughtful, as well as kind and just.

Half an hour later I'd left the husband and wife hugging each other on the step of their cottage. Both were crying with joy, and I was struck again by how terribly Mrs Chichester must have suffered and how unfair her imprisonment had been.

Back at Johnson's house, Tom Ward was still in the cellar; he was talking to the witch in the sixth cell on the right. Her name was Gwen Raddle, and I couldn't abide her. She was always picking her nose and spitting onto her left shoe. I spied Old Henry busily slopping out the cells, muttering to himself as he did so. Tom had clearly wasted no time in bringing him here.

Catching sight of me, Tom came towards the stairs and beckoned for me to follow. We went up into the kitchen, and I saw tomato soup simmering in a pan on the stove – he *had* been busy! He gestured for me to sit down, then ladled it into two bowls and brought them across to the table.

He talked between mouthfuls. 'Do you mind if I ask you a few questions, Wulf? If I get too nosy, just tell me to mind my own business!' he said with a grin. 'First of all, how old are you?'

'I'm fourteen,' I told him. 'I'll be fifteen next year – on the sixteenth of February.'

Tom whistled under his breath. 'I thought you were older. I don't mean your size – you've got a bit of growing to do yet – I mean in your manner and speech. You've got an old head on your young shoulders, that's for sure.'

I smiled, pleased at the compliment.

He went on with his questions: 'How long have you been a monk, Wulf? And how much time have you spent working for Johnson?' he wanted to know.

'My noviciate began nearly a year ago, and I've been with Spook Johnson for six weeks,' I replied.

Tom considered this for a moment. When he spoke again, he sounded thoughtful. 'I've been wondering about you, Wulf. You know you told me that Johnson had specified certain criteria for the monk who was going to write his book? Do you have any idea what they were?'

I shrugged. 'As I told you, the Abbot didn't say—'

'Have a guess,' he interrupted. 'What do you think they might have been?'

I considered the question for a moment. 'He'd have wanted someone whose penmanship was good. That would be important,' I said.

'Of course. And how many monks are there in your abbey, Wulf?' Tom asked.

'Eighty-four, including five noviciates. Eighty-three, now that I've left.'

'So, you were the best scribe out of all of them – the pick of the whole bunch?'

I felt my face start to go red. 'I don't know about that. I think I was probably picked because I don't just copy what I see. I use my imagination. As I told you, the Abbot warned me about that. You need imagination to write a book about Spook Johnson's exploits – a lot of it!' I added with a smile.

But Tom Ward's next question wiped that smile off my face.

'You see ghosts, don't you?'

My heart began to hammer in my chest and bile rose up into my throat. I lurched to my feet, struggling to breathe, the world spinning about me. I'd never told anyone about that terrifying part of my life – how had Tom known? I wondered. I'd omitted it from my accounts – but I knew I couldn't lie to him outright.

'Yes,' I said, my voice hardly more than a whisper. I felt sick, and scared.

Tom stood up and reached across the table, putting a hand firmly on each of my shoulders.

'Take deep slow breaths, Wulf,' he said. 'You'll feel better soon . . .'

I did as he advised, and my heart began to slow. He gestured for me to sit back down.

'I'm sorry to startle you, Wulf. Such powers are nothing to worry about, once you know how to control them,' he told me kindly. 'That takes time, and I'd like to help you if I can. However, right now we've got a job to do, so any useful advice I might give you will have to wait. And I don't want to upset you further tonight. We'll let it drop for now. All right?'

I nodded, grateful. And Tom was right – for now, we had to focus on rescuing Johnson.

He returned to the matter at hand. 'So – Gwen Raddle, the witch I was talking to just now – she isn't so very dangerous. If she agrees to the deal I'm going to offer her, I'll let her go.'

What sort of deal was it? I wondered, realizing that he was forming another alliance with one of Hell's servants. I was amazed he felt he could trust them.

Tom swallowed a mouthful of soup and then answered my unspoken question. 'Firstly, Gwen Raddle specializes in love potions and suchlike, which sounds harmless enough, though people are paying to control someone else. A man wants someone else's wife. The witch takes a payment and gets her for him. It can be used to break up families. From that she makes a good living, and Johnson was right to put her in that cell. But in return for her promise not to do it again, I'll free her.'

'Won't she just carry on the same as before?' I asked.

'Probably,' Tom replied, 'but at least I'll have given her a second chance. Everybody – well, almost everybody – deserves that. Besides, there'll be another condition tied to her release. What we are going up against seems to be very dangerous. To bend those bars like that took incredible strength. Even water witches aren't as strong as that. My instinct tells me that this is something from the dark that is totally new. So I'm going to borrow one of Spook Johnson's tactics. I'm going to use Gwen Raddle as bait.'

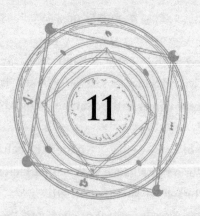

11

GWEN RADDLE

In spite of Tom's talk of having a job to do, he delayed our rescue attempt once again. For some reason he wanted to wait until the sun went down. This procrastination was the only thing I didn't like about him. Didn't he know that it was the thief of time? Couldn't he see that the situation was urgent? Why was he being so cautious?

'Isn't it better to go up against one of Hell's servants in daylight?' I protested politely. 'Aren't they stronger during the hours of darkness?'

He nodded. 'That's sometimes true, Wulf, but occasionally you have to fight the dark with darkness,' he said cryptically. 'The witch won't expect us to make our move after dark, when she's at her strongest. The element of surprise might tip the balance in our favour.'

So we waited until dusk, and then the three of us set off for the village, Tom gripping the witch firmly by her left forearm. I walked a little behind them. Gwen Raddle smelled really bad. I don't know how he could bear to be so close to her.

By now the drizzle had stopped, the sky had partly cleared and the full moon was out; but the grass was slippery and the ground soft underfoot. At last we reached the south-facing slope that afforded a view of the village. Moonlight bathed the wood, the main street and the houses in a silver sheen. I could see the shop clearly. The village still seemed to be deserted.

'Right then, Gwen, this is what I'd like you to do. Go down to that shop,' Tom said, pointing it out, 'and ask if you can talk to the Spook who's been captured. Say you've escaped from the cells underneath Johnson's house and want to give him a piece of your mind. But if the witch does let you meet him, don't hurt him. Is that clear?'

'Hurt him? Why would I hurt my good friend Mr Johnson?' Gwen asked, her harsh voice heavy with sarcasm.

Tom gave her his wolfish grin. 'Well, if you do, it'll be back in that cell for you, and you'll never see the light of day again.' She paled, and he went on: 'If you do see him, carry on down the main street. Once you're clear of the village, we'll circle round and meet up with you to find out what you've learned. I want to know where he's being held, what condition he's in and how he's being guarded. Understand?'

Gwen nodded her head, though she was clearly reluctant, and he released her arm. She took a step backwards and stared at him as she rooted up her nose with her forefinger. 'Got to make it convincing though, haven't I?' she said, before examining something impaled on the end of her fingernail and popping it into her mouth. 'I'll curse at him for five minutes, slap his cheeks a bit, then spit into his face – that should do it, and I'll feel better afterwards. Then I'll meet you yonder!' she said, pointing east before spitting something slimy onto her pointy left shoe.

Tom let her go about thirty paces down the hill before setting off. We moved slowly into the small wood behind the houses, and reached its lower edge just in time to see Gwen knocking on the door of the village shop.

'Do you trust her?' I asked. 'She is a witch, after all. She might give us away.'

'That's true,' Tom said, keeping his voice low. 'It's usually best not to trust a witch, but sometimes, as my master taught me, you just have to take a chance and rely on your instincts. My gut feeling is that Gwen Raddle won't betray us.'

Everything was still and quiet, and the raps on the door echoed off the hillside.

'Hopefully she'll be taken to the place where Johnson's being held. That's when we go in and release him,' Tom continued. 'Of course, he could simply be in the shop. In that case, we'll give it a few moments and go in.'

So Tom Ward had never intended to meet up with Gwen Raddle afterwards! As he'd suggested earlier, he was just using her as a distraction to cover his attack. I was impressed by his ingenuity – if a little taken aback by how callously he'd used Gwen as bait.

'I see. And what if the witch uses Hell magic against you?' I asked nervously.

'Well, I told you that spooks are always seventh sons of seventh sons,' Tom replied, his voice now a whisper, 'and that gives me *some* immunity against witchcraft. That and the element of surprise should be enough.'

I said nothing, though I wasn't convinced. Spook Johnson's immunity hadn't been very effective, I reflected. But then I reassured myself with the thought that he'd been drunk and probably unconscious when he was taken.

Below us the door opened and Gwen Raddle went into the shop. When it closed behind her, time seemed to stand still. Everything was quiet, and nothing moved on the street below. Then, after what seemed an eternity, Tom came to his feet and beckoned to me.

He'd hardly taken a step when we heard a terrible noise, and came to a sudden halt. It sounded as if a giant had exhaled a huge lungful of air. The moon was obscured by a cloud, but I could still see the outline of the village houses. Tom seemed to be staring at the roof of the shop, his gaze fixed upon the chimney.

Then there were other noises. At first they reminded me of my encounter with the stone-chucker boggart: it seemed as if small pebbles were falling down into the grass. I thought at first it might be rain – something was splashing against my cheek and forehead. Next I heard larger, heavier things dropping through the branches above.

I didn't realize immediately that it was pieces of Gwen Raddle falling from the sky.

It seemed that Tom had understood because, when something very large fell at our feet, rather than recoil in revulsion as I did, he went down on his knees and angled his ear close, as if listening to something.

I saw at last that it was the witch's severed head, glowing a sickly green. It had wide staring eyes, an open mouth, and a nose that Gwen could no longer pick because her arms and hands had fallen elsewhere.

I felt sick and turned away, but then felt compelled to look again. To my horror, I realized that the lips were moving and the eyes had opened even wider; they seemed to be staring at me.

'What happened, Gwen?' Tom was saying. 'Who did this to you?'

I thought he must be crazy: how could such a thing, separated from all that kept it conscious, be able to talk? Surely the witch's soul had moved on, probably falling into the darkest, foulest pit in Hell?

The lips moved again, but no words could be heard. After a moment they were still, and Tom rose to his feet.

He turned to face me. 'The head of a witch can live on for a few moments after it's been separated from the body,' he explained. 'It can't make sounds, but you can sometimes read the lips and work out what is being said. Unfortunately, Gwen wasn't able to communicate anything sensible.'

Tom paced up and down in front of the head for a moment, deep in thought. Then he reached into his bag and produced a pen and a piece of paper. He rested it on the back of a notebook and began to write. It seemed to be quite a long message, and it was several minutes before he folded it carefully three times and handed it to me.

'I want you to go to Johnson's house and wait for me there,' he said. 'If I'm not back by dawn, please take this to Chipenden and give it to Alice.'

'But why? The only reason you'd give this to me is if . . .' Realization dawned on me. 'You don't think you'll succeed, do you?' I asked. 'You think you'll end up a prisoner like Johnson, or worse—'

'I'm just being cautious, that's all,' interrupted Tom. 'Most likely I'll be fine. But there's no point in you staying here, where you're in danger. I've never seen anything like this before. Some power has blasted Gwen to pieces, and made her head fall precisely at my feet. I think we're up against something really powerful – something unknown – and I don't want to take any chances.'

'And what good will this note do? Does Alice know of someone else who could help you?' I asked.

He closed his eyes and seemed to ponder what I'd said. 'I'm not sure if there's anything she could do. We didn't part on the best of terms, but she deserves to know what has happened to me – if it comes to that, and I'm not saying it will. So, will you do it?'

I nodded. How could I refuse?

'One more thing,' Tom continued, and his voice took on a warning tone. 'What I've written is private. Something between me and Alice. Will you promise not to read it? Promise to place it unread into her hands?'

'Yes, I promise,' I told him, and I meant it.

'Then off you go, Wulf. I'll wait until you're clear before I go down to the village.'

'Are you sure you wouldn't rather I stayed?' I asked. I felt bad about leaving him alone, though I wasn't sure what help I'd be.

He smiled. 'I'm sure, Wulf. It's important that you're free to deliver that note just in case things go wrong. There's no point in us both being captured.'

I nodded, then set off back up the hill. Once I reached the summit I glanced back. Tom was still staring at me. I waved, then picked up my pace and set off towards Salford. As I walked, I prayed for him.

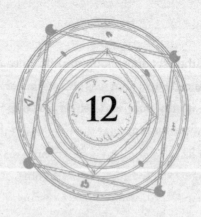

12

THE QUISITOR

Once back at Spook Johnson's house, I went down to the cellar to check on the witches.

They were quiet. Most of them were asleep, and the two still awake did no more than stare at me with hostile eyes. The cells had been cleaned out and Old Henry had left.

I could have gone up to my room and tried to sleep, but I was anxious and could only pace up and down the kitchen. I kept hoping that I'd hear a knock at the door and it would be Tom Ward. Even better, if I heard a key turn, I'd know it was both of them, since Johnson always carried his bunch of house keys in his pocket. After a while I sat down on a chair. I felt weary beyond belief and, in spite of my anxiety, soon fell asleep.

*

The next thing I knew it was morning, with bright sunlight streaming through the windows.

I immediately felt sick with worry. What could have happened to Tom? I'd promised him that I'd set off for Chipenden if he didn't return by dawn, but I decided to give him a bit longer. A few hours wouldn't hurt, surely? There was still a chance that he might have rescued Johnson, and for all I knew he was already on his way back from the village. It wouldn't do to cause unnecessary upset to this Alice. So I decided to make breakfast and wait.

Johnson paid Old Henry to keep the food cupboards stocked, but he hadn't been doing a very good job. The first egg I cracked open was rotten and stank out the whole kitchen. There wasn't much else to eat, so I had to content myself with chewing on a few dry strips of salted beef.

I waited until almost noon before deciding that I could hang on no longer. I took a hunk of stale cheese, stuffed it in my pocket and readied myself to leave for Chipenden. I decided to call at Old Henry's first to tell him to keep looking after the witches in the cellar and to get some fresh food in.

As it turned out, I didn't need to. He came to me.

I heard a key turning in the lock and rushed to the front door, thinking it might be Johnson and Tom. But it was Old Henry who met my eyes with a sly grin.

'He's here, my lord!' he shouted. 'Just as I told you!'

Confused, I looked over his shoulder – and saw a large group of people in the street before me. One of them was on horseback, the others on foot, and although they were all dressed like monks, they carried spears, with clubs and swords at their belts. I also recognized a couple of unarmed monks from the abbey. One of them was Brother Halsall, the monk in charge of noviciates.

He stared at me, then strode towards the door and, quite roughly, pushed Henry aside. The old man protested loudly, but Halsall ignored him, and grabbed me, speaking into my ear, his voice hardly more than a whisper.

'Obey every instruction of the Quisitor without question, Brother Beowulf. I'll try to help you if I can, but you are in danger of suffering extreme punishment.'

It was then that I realized who the big man on the black horse was. It was Father Ormskirk, the Quisitor, who took his orders directly from the new Bishop of Blackburn. He was responsible for trying and burning witches. But what had I done? I wondered fearfully. Why was I in danger? And what were they going to do to me?

They didn't bind me with ropes – but, anyway, there was no need. I was marched back to the abbey surrounded by armed monks, with the Quisitor leading the way on his big black horse; I had no chance of escape.

The journey only took a couple of hours, but it seemed much longer. My head was whirling with thoughts. I didn't think I'd done anything wrong. After all, the Abbot had ordered me to work for Spook Johnson – and I'd been trying to help free an innocent man from the clutches of Hell.

However, I'd heard about the new Bishop of Blackburn – enough to worry me greatly. The monks had gossiped about him: some didn't like the way he went about things, but others were enthusiastic and supported his zeal. He aimed to increase the wealth of the Church whenever possible, and wanted to root out all Hell's creatures – especially witches. He had declared his intention to appoint three new quisitors, Matthew Ormskirk being the first, to help him in his task. He was on a mission – and I just had to hope I wasn't in his way.

When we reached the abbey, the monks searched me and, to my dismay, confiscated the letter that Tom had asked me to give to Alice. Now I'd let him down twice over.

Then they marched me up to one of the cells reserved for noviciates during their first week at the abbey. It was very spartan, with bare walls, a wooden bench to sleep on, and an open window through which cold air gusted. This was to give us young monks a taste of the new life we had embarked upon, and quickly wean us away from our home comforts. After a week we were moved into cells that were slightly more comfortable. It worked: I remember feeling very grateful for the improvement.

However, there was one difference now. The first time I'd slept in a cell here, I could have opened the door any time I liked. Now it was locked and bolted on the outside. It had become a prison cell. There were no bars on the window, but it offered no means of escape. I could never have squeezed my shoulders through the long narrow frame, and besides, there was a long drop to the rocky hillside.

So I sat on my bench and waited. No doubt they were going to question me, but I still couldn't understand what I'd done.

After about an hour the door was unlocked and Brother Halsall came in. He closed the door and stood facing me, a slight frown on his face. I started to come to my feet, but he waved me back down.

'Rest, Brother Beowulf. You'll need all your strength for the ordeal that lies ahead of you.' I slumped lower on my bench, and he shook his head and sighed deeply. 'We would like to help you, but I'm afraid there is very little we can do. While the Quisitor resides in the abbey, he is the representative of the Bishop, and therefore the supreme authority here. Even the Abbot cannot intervene.'

'But what have I done wrong, Brother Halsall?' I asked. 'I simply carried out the tasks that I was set by the Abbot. I was writing an account of Spook Johnson's life, gathering information about his methods of dealing with the dark. That's exactly what I was ordered to do.'

He ignored my protests. 'The Quisitor will interrogate you and record everything you learned of those dark practices. It will be in your own interests to supply as much information as you can – that might soften your eventual punishment. It may, indeed, save you from burning.'

The word 'burning' shocked me to the core. Surely I'd done nothing to deserve that!

'I don't understand! Why am I to be punished, Brother Halsall? I've done nothing other than what was demanded of me by the Abbot.'

Brother Halsall frowned. 'This is untrue, Brother Beowulf. Why did you go north to visit another spook when Johnson was taken by that creature from Hell? You should have returned to the abbey immediately and informed us of the situation. That was your duty.'

'But Spook Johnson was in mortal danger!' I exclaimed. 'I thought the best way of saving him was to go and seek help from another spook, an expert in such matters. If Johnson died, how could I have continued with my appointed task? And every minute I delayed increased the risk that he would be slain – so I headed straight for Tom Ward.'

Now Brother Halsall was angry. 'You were given special dispensation to work with *one* spook – not two! Not only that; you consorted with a spook who is clearly living with a witch. As soon as Henry Miller told us that Johnson had been taken, and that you and Ward were in cahoots, the

Abbot sent for the Quisitor. I doubt he will give much credence to your explanation, but I do have some good news for you – the Quisitor has decided to try one of Johnson's witches before dealing with you. That means you have a few days before your interrogation begins. In that time you will be given only a small amount of bread and a little water – the Abbot has decided that you should fast, and pray for your soul.'

With that, Brother Halsall left me. His words shocked and frightened me. Until now I'd thought this was all a mistake – the Quisitor would quickly see that I was innocent of any wrongdoing. But now, for the first time, I was truly scared. I didn't know what Tom had written in his letter, but it had been enough for them to work out that Alice was a witch. I had sought help from a man who was living with her. That was certain to go against me.

Even a monk could be tortured and burned if the Quisitor thought his crime deserved it. It was believed that burning purified the sinner, and allowed his soul to escape Hell.

I'd never even considered this when travelling to Chipenden to get help from Tom Ward. After all, I had already decided to leave the abbey. I no longer wished to be a monk. I had even decided that I didn't believe in God.

Now it was too late and I was in extreme danger.

I knelt down on the cold flagged floor and began to pray.

*

It was difficult to sleep in such a cold cell, with my belly rumbling with hunger. There was no breakfast the following morning, and my hunger increased; it felt as if rats were gnawing at my insides. Even worse, my mouth became dry with thirst, my tongue beginning to swell.

At midday I was given the only sustenance that I was to receive before my interrogation – a dry crust of bread and a small jug of water. It was meagre fare, but I gulped it down as if it were a great feast.

So imagine my surprise when, the following morning, I found things much improved for my interrogation. I was escorted along to a small room and told to sit down at a table opposite the Quisitor; before me was placed a large bowl of porridge and a steaming cup of herb tea.

'Eat and drink, Brother Beowulf!' he commanded. 'Take your time. When you are finished, I will begin the questioning.'

Father Ormskirk was a big man with a broad, florid face and bushy eyebrows. I had seen him once, two months earlier, when he first visited the abbey. Then his gaze had been stern and his expression grim. Now I gazed at him in astonishment. He was actually smiling at me.

I thanked him and began to eat. Throughout my meal I could feel his eyes fixed upon my face, but he did not speak another word. So close was his scrutiny that it made me feel uncomfortable – but not so much that it spoiled my appetite!

Never had porridge tasted so good. After I had eaten it all and drained the cup of tea, the Quisitor clapped his hands, and a monk called Brother Xavier came and took away the bowl and cup. I tried to catch his eye, but he ignored me. Then another monk entered; one I did not recognize. He was a tall, pale, gaunt-looking man of about forty, his eyes set very close together.

'This is Brother Sabden, my assistant,' said Father Ormskirk as the new monk took a seat on his left. 'He is an executioner and also an expert in torturing sinners and bringing them to repentance. He has slain many souls and saved an equal number. But today it is his skill with the pen that will be put to use. He is here to record all that you have learned about the dark practices of spooks.'

I glanced at Brother Sabden and a sudden chill ran down my spine. He did not even look at me, but he radiated malevolence. I realized that if I were found guilty, this was the monk who would torture and eventually kill me.

'Let us begin, Brother Beowulf. List and describe the dark magical practices that Spook Johnson used in his dealings with witches,' the Quisitor ordered.

Full of fear about what might soon befall me, I was only too happy to oblige. 'When confronting a witch, he would bind her with a silver chain,' I began. 'He worked at this skill several times a week in order to maintain it. The chain was cast into the air from his left hand so that it fell upon the witch—'

'Ha! The left hand!' cried Father Ormskirk, evidently pleased at what I'd just told him.

'The intention was to achieve what spooks call "spread", where the binding extends from the knees to the mouth,' I continued. 'It is particularly important that the chain wraps around the mouth so that the bound witch cannot utter spells.'

'Make a special note of that, Brother Sabden,' said the Quisitor, turning to his colleague. 'The use of the left hand is no doubt a vital part of the magical ritual of binding.'

The Church considered anyone favouring their left hand, which they called the *sinistral*, was in league with the Devil. As it happened, I was ambidextrous and could use either hand equally well. But, knowing what the Church would think of this, I always used my right hand lest suspicion fall on me.

The questioning continued and I explained that spooks used a rowan staff, as this particular wood caused pain and revulsion in a witch, and that they set a silver-alloy blade in the end of the staff to kill or disable a witch.

As I spoke, I felt a vague sense of guilt at giving away so many secrets about the way spooks practised their trade. However, I was in grave danger, and very afraid of what might happen to me.

But as I continued, I gradually saw the pleasant expression on the Quisitor's face fade, to be replaced by frustration, and even growing anger. I was puzzled but kept talking, unable to work out what was wrong.

Finally he interrupted me and spoke harshly.

'All this is about the practical skills of dealing with witches. What about the demonic magic employed by spooks? Did you ever hear Johnson recite the Lord's Prayer backwards? Did he use blood or milk, or any parts of animals?'

I shook my head. 'No, Father, I never witnessed such things. He used only those skills that I have told you about,' I said, frowning in confusion.

'Perhaps he was too subtle for you. Spells can be uttered under the breath,' he pointed out. 'But did you not search the books in his library, as you were instructed?'

'I did, Father, many times. However, there were hundreds of books, and only rarely was I left alone in the house. I had time to dip into a few dozen – that's all. I found nothing relating to spooks using magic.'

'Are you *really* trying to tell me that you found nothing?' Father Ormskirk exclaimed angrily. 'I find that hard to believe! Well, my servants are now studying Spook Johnson's library. I predict that they will succeed where you failed.'

He was shouting now, his eyes bulging from their sockets, his face turning red. I kept talking quickly in an attempt to assuage his anger.

'There were many accounts of the methodology of using Hell magic, but only with regard to that used by witches,' I said, somewhat desperately. 'For example, they employ spells of glamour and—'

'Enough!' shouted the Quisitor, banging his fist down on the table. 'I am extremely disappointed, Brother Beowulf. I had hoped that you would be able to help us in our task of countering the Devil's works – and that the knowledge you passed on would lessen the punishment that I must inflict upon your body for the good of your soul. You have learned nothing! Therefore you will now be returned to your cell, and we will address your trespasses at dawn tomorrow.'

With that, I was taken away, trembling with fear. In my cell, however, something awaited me that made things far worse.

I realized I could smell burning. Smoke was blowing past the open window, and gusts of wind forced it in towards me. There were sounds in the distance too: raucous shouts, and then someone screaming in agony.

I peered through the narrow cell window, the acrid smoke stinging my eyes, but could see nothing. Whatever was happening was out of sight, somewhere west of the abbey on the grassy field between the building and the river.

Suddenly I identified the source of the smoke.

They were burning one of the witches.

13

THE BEAST IS COMING

Soon after dawn the next day I was taken to be questioned again. This time Father Ormskirk did not greet me with a smile; nor was I fed porridge. I wasn't hungry anyway: my stomach knotted in terror when two monks took me, not into the same room, but into a large cellar somewhere below the abbey. It stank of sweat and blood, and the Quisitor was standing by the door with folded arms and a forbidding expression.

There were torches hanging on the walls, and a brazier in the corner glowing with orange heat. Then I saw, with a jolt of shock, a long table with cylinders at either end; attached to these were straps and ropes. It was a rack – a torture device for stretching a human body so far that joints eventually popped out of their sockets.

Next to this was a metal table; the copper tray upon it was set with what I immediately recognized as instruments of torture: a pair of pliers, and long, sharp needles that I knew were used to test women to see if they were witches. Their points were jabbed into the flesh again and again, causing the victim extreme pain. However, if they plunged the needles in and there was no reaction, it was concluded that the Devil's mark had been found, and the woman was a witch. Then she was taken and burned. Were they going to do that to me? I wondered, my legs trembling with fear.

Looking around the chamber, I reflected that Kersal Abbey was very large – I was not familiar with every corner. I'd certainly known nothing of this underground torture room. How long had it been here, awaiting the pleasure of the Quisitor and Brother Sabden?

The monks forced me down onto a metal chair, and fastened straps tightly round my arms, chest and legs to bind me. I noticed then that a thin steel rod was set deep in the brazier, its end lost among the glowing coals. Fear caused beads of sweat to form on my brow and flow down into my eyes. Were they going to burn me now?

The monks left me alone with the Quisitor, who remained silent, but then Brother Sabden entered the chamber. He came over and looked down at me, his eyes cold in his narrow face; it was as if I were some pest that needed to be exterminated. His sleeves were rolled up and he wore a long leather apron. He was carrying two glass jars.

Father Ormskirk gave me a grim smile, his face twisted into a travesty of humour, but his eyes were as sharp as flint and as cruel as death.

'Show Brother Beowulf the jars,' he instructed.

Brother Sabden placed the larger one on the table and held the smaller close to my face.

'What do you see?' the Quisitor asked quietly, walking forward to stand beside his assistant.

I began to shake; I couldn't keep my body still. The jar was full of teeth. Some were long canines, others smaller; some were white, while others were yellow or brown. They all looked human.

'Some of those we question are very brave,' continued the Quisitor. 'The Devil gives his own creatures courage. We counter that with endurance. Most human mouths have thirty-two teeth. Imagine the agony as each is drawn forth! And each tooth can take over an hour to extract.' He gave a horrid smile as he saw my fearful face. 'Now show Brother Beowulf the large jar.'

Brother Sabden held it up to my eyes and I saw things floating around in a milky liquid. I felt sick.

'This jar contains eyeballs and tongues, Brother Beowulf. So why don't you use those eyes of yours to read this and employ that tongue of yours to answer my questions,' Father Ormskirk said.

He unfolded a piece of paper and held it close to my face. I quickly realized that it was the letter Tom Ward had given me to take to Alice.

I'm so sorry, Alice, but if this note is placed in your hands it means that I've bitten off more than I can chew and we will probably never see each other again.

I thought I was doing what I'd been trained to do - and that my duty as a spook was to protect the County. At the time I truly believed that had to take precedence over all other things. But now I realize that I was wrong. My greater duty was to you. During the journey I've had ample time to think, and I now know that I should have stayed by your side as you asked me. You begged me to stay for the birth and I turned my back on you. I'm so sorry for doing that.

So I am writing to apologize for what I did and to tell you that I love you. I will always love you, Alice. But please don't try to help me. If you are reading this, I believe that I will already be beyond help. I also believe that we are facing something from the dark that is new - a dangerous and powerful entity. It took Spook Johnson as if he were no more than a child rather than a formidable spook with years of experience, and I have just seen further evidence that is a testament to its terrible power.

So please stay in Chipenden. By now I know that you will have given birth to our child. So please do not place yourself in danger by coming here. Without your magic it would be hopeless, and even if your power does return, do not put yourself at risk. You will be a good mother to our child, the best protector that it could ever have. That is your duty now. Put that first. I did the wrong thing, so please don't follow in my footsteps.

I love you,

Tom

'Isn't it touching?' the Quisitor said sarcastically. 'He clearly cares about the witch – about her and the brat which by now must have been spawned from her dark womb. And this is the evidence that damns *you*, Brother Beowulf. Not only did you step beyond your remit and seek the help of another spook; you were prepared to return to the lair of that witch to carry his message. Do you confess your sins and beg forgiveness?' he demanded.

I was afraid, but I wanted to defend myself. 'I did not intend any sin, Father. If I sinned, I sinned in ignorance. I simply went to seek help that only another spook could give. I intended no harm.'

'No *harm*? No *harm*! Brother Beowulf, you did *great* harm to your own soul,' he exclaimed in outrage. 'We believe that you are hiding things from us. We believe that you did indeed discover the rituals and secrets used by spooks, the dark powers they use to carry out their abominable trade. But, because you have allied yourself with them, you refuse to give us the evidence we require. By the way – what did happen to the Spook called Ward? Where is he to be found?'

'I don't know what happened to him, Father,' I replied. 'I left him at an abandoned village; he was about to go in search of Spook Johnson. He told me to leave him and, if he wasn't back by dawn, to go to Chipenden with that note.'

'How interesting. We have searched the village. Henry Miller guided us there, but we found nothing. The place was deserted. It must be years since it was last occupied. Perhaps you do know where he is to be found but prefer to protect him?' Father Ormskirk suggested.

'No, Father! I'm telling the truth, I swear—'

'We shall see. I believe you are only fourteen years of age, Brother Beowulf. That makes you little more than a child. However, you are a noviciate monk, and with that comes a special responsibility to aid us in rooting out evil. I do not inflict pain lightly, but we will show no regard for your tender years. We do what we do in order to defeat the Devil, and although pain will torment your flesh, it will bring about your confession and cleanse your soul.'

The Quisitor signalled to Brother Sabden, who walked across to the brazier and pulled out the rod. It had a small oblong piece of metal at the end and it was glowing red. He came slowly towards me.

'We will begin your true interrogation tomorrow,' Father Ormskirk told me. 'So tonight you must pray. You must make peace with your Creator. Your body may be doomed, but your eternal soul can still escape Hell. And in order to help you focus your mind, we will give you a foretaste of the pain that awaits you tomorrow . . .'

With the speed of a striking snake, Brother Sabden grabbed my hair, forced my head against the chair back – then pressed the end of the glowing rod down hard against my forehead. There was a burning pressure, a sizzling sound and a hiss of steam. I knew that he had burned my forehead, but I felt nothing.

He released my head and I stared up at him in shock. For a few seconds more there was no pain . . . and then it hit me with an intensity that made me cry out. Brother Sabden smiled in satisfaction, but the Quisitor just nodded at me and then left the chamber. The two monks returned, unfastened the straps and half carried me back to my cell.

By then I was no longer screaming, but the pain was unbearable and I was moaning and blubbering like a baby. If this was only a foretaste of what was to come tomorrow, what terrible, terrible torments awaited me?

I couldn't sleep, and the pain went on and on, long after dark. At some point during the night Brother Halsall came into my cell and put his arm round my shoulders, raising me to a sitting position.

'Drink this. It will help you to sleep,' he said, bringing a cup to my lips.

The liquid was bitter, but it slid down my throat and instantly warmed my stomach.

He looked at my forehead. 'That's a very nasty burn,' he said, 'but this should ease the pain.'

He smeared a cold ointment on it, then left me alone in my cell.

I did sleep a little, although the pain kept waking me up.

The third time I awoke I felt the coldness. Not only was it there in the darkest corner of the cells, it was also moving up and down my spine, telling me that one of Hell's creatures was very close.

The room was again filled with that pale yellow light – and there above me on the ceiling were the flickering shadows that I knew so well, as if moonlight were passing through a tree's bare branches.

Slowly, as my heart began to race with fear, those shadows resolved themselves into a human form; into the faceless demon.

My situation was very bad. I was in pain, and in the morning I faced torture and death. It seemed that things had now got even worse. I was filled with terror at the coming of the demon and the thought of the fresh pain he might inflict upon me.

'Get behind me, Demon! Leave me! Go from this place – I command thee!' I cried desperately.

'But you need me now more than ever, Brother Beowulf!' it cried. *'I bring you good tidings. If you can endure one more day, you will be free and beyond the ministrations of those cruel priests. The beast is coming to save you – the beast with two heads!'*

I didn't know what to believe. As far as I knew, the demon had never lied to me, but how could I give credence to its words – even if they were words which told of my escape?

'Why would such a beast help me?' I demanded.

'The beast has reasons of its own. It will require something from you in payment. But in order to be saved there are two things that you must do. Firstly, you must use your wits in order to survive tomorrow's trials. Secondly, on the following day you must persuade the priests to take you outside these walls. There among the trees and meadows the beast will be all powerful and able to help you.'

'And how am I supposed to do that?' I asked bitterly.

'*Think!*' commanded the demon; then it sighed in what sounded like exasperation. '*Use your imagination!*'

The word 'imagination' made me recall what the Abbot had said to me when telling me off about writing my own accounts: *Imagination belongs to God. It is not for us poor humans to attempt to exercise that faculty.* I had used my own words rather than just copying existing text. The Abbot had warned me that it was a sin, and now this demon was tempting me to employ my imagination again. With what sounded like a satisfied chuckle, the image on the ceiling faded, and I was left alone with my thoughts. There were a lot of them. They whirled around my head so fast that I did not sleep again that night.

The following morning, my forehead still throbbing with the pain of the burn, I was taken to the torture chamber again. The Quisitor and Brother Sabden were waiting for me. I was dragged towards the chair, but as they began to strap me in I called out to them:

'I am ready to confess!'

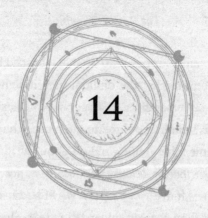

14

A STRONG DISLIKE OF QUISITORS

'Ah! A confession!' The Quisitor gave a cruel smile as the monks continued to strap me tightly to the metal chair. 'I am listening, Brother Beowulf. I will give you a minute at the most before Brother Sabden begins his work. But please do not waste my time.'

Brother Sabden approached me. He was holding a small pair of pliers and looking hungrily at my mouth. It seemed he intended to begin by extracting my teeth. I began to sweat with fear.

Since the demon's visit I'd lain awake, thinking desperately, planning exactly what to say. Despite the short time that he had allowed me, I started with a question.

'Father, have your servants found anything in Spook Johnson's books about his magical practices and rituals?'

Father Ormskirk shook his head. 'Not so far, but there are many books and the process will take time. You have offered to confess. Are you able to save our valuable time and indicate where in the books of that library such information is to be found?'

'No, Father, because nothing is written down in those books,' I told him. 'Spooks do not record such secret information. They store it all in their memories, and now some of it is stored in mine.'

'And are you now prepared to divulge those secrets?'

'Yes, Father.'

The Quisitor hastily sat down, then gestured to Brother Sabden, who reluctantly returned the pliers to the tray, then sat down next to him and picked up a pen. As he dipped it into the inkwell, he looked more than a little disappointed.

The monks unfastened the leather straps and I came to my feet, my legs trembling.

'Take a seat, Brother Beowulf, and begin,' commanded the Quisitor, pointing to the chair that stood opposite him. I did so, then took a deep breath before speaking.

'One important spell used by Spook Johnson is called *maximus*. It is similar to the spell of *glamour*, frequently employed by witches when an old and ugly face and body can be made to appear beautiful and alluring. However, in the case of a spook, the intention is to make the user of the spell appear larger and more ferocious. When used against witches, it renders them terrified and bewildered, thus making it easier to bind them with a silver chain.'

'Good. Very good, Brother Beowulf!' Father Ormskirk said, giving me a smile while Brother Sabden wrote down what I'd said. 'Do you know the words of the spell?'

I shook my head. 'Johnson muttered the words under his breath.'

'A pity – but continue with your account.'

Wasting no time, I went on to name spells for binding boggarts or driving them away, and for dealing with lingering ghosts. I talked quickly, telling lie after lie. Telling such untruths was against everything I believed in, but I was terrified of being tortured. I would say or do anything to avoid such pain.

The Quisitor didn't ask me to slow down, and I had the satisfaction of watching Brother Sabden struggle to keep up with my flow of words.

Then I paused and prepared to embark upon the second part of my deception.

'Of course, the spells don't work without the charms,' I said.

'Charms? Do you mean amulets, Brother Beowulf? Are they crafted from iron, silver or wood?' Father Ormskirk's voice was eager.

'They are bone charms, Father, imbued with Hell magic. Some are bones taken from the newly dead at midnight, filched from freshly dug graves.'

'Tell me, Brother Beowulf, did you participate in such thefts?' he asked.

I shook my head. 'The necessary items are gathered close to the winter solstice,' I lied smoothly. 'Spook Johnson has a cache of them that will last him many years.'

'Where is this cache to be found?' the Quisitor pressed eagerly. 'Is it hidden in his house?'

'He never keeps the charms in one location for long – they're too valuable,' I said, continuing with my pretence. 'He moves them from place to place. At the moment they are in an abandoned farmhouse. I could take you there tomorrow and show you their hiding place . . .'

Father Ormskirk stared at me for a long time. 'Is it far from here?' he asked.

'No – not much more than two hours' walk,' I replied.

'Then why wait until tomorrow? We will go directly after lunch, Brother Beowulf!' he exclaimed triumphantly.

My heart sank. I had done well – better than I expected, in fact – and the Quisitor had believed everything I'd said. But now I had made a big mistake. I should have pretended that the charms were hidden a long way from Salford. Then we would have needed to prepare provisions, which would have taken time. According to the demon, my opportunity to be rescued was tomorrow, not today.

Not only had I failed in potentially saving my own skin, I now realized that, if the Quisitor believed my account, Tom

Ward and Spook Johnson would now be in terrible danger –
if indeed they ever managed to escape from the witch.

I had plenty of time to think about this as the monks
returned me to my cell to await the Quisitor's further pleasure.
The sky was bright blue and there wasn't a cloud in the sky.
But, as I stared out of the high window, to my astonishment I
saw that it had begun to rain. Within moments it had grown
into a torrential downpour, obscuring my view of the rocky
hillside and driving straight through the open window. I had
to retreat to the far corner of the cell to avoid getting wet.

After about an hour the rain eased a little, but it still
showed no sign of ending. The sky was now dark grey as far
as the horizon.

I heard a key turning in the lock and Brother Halsall came
into my cell. After silently examining the burn on my
forehead, he rubbed fresh ointment into it.

'No doubt you will be delighted to hear that you will
receive a hot evening meal,' he told me. Then he gave me
even better news. Because of the bad weather, the Quisitor
had postponed our visit to the abandoned farm until
tomorrow. I was saved!

We set off mid-morning. The sky was clear and the sun
warm on our heads as we headed east towards the farm.

The Quisitor led the way, riding high on his black horse. I
walked just to his left, with Brother Sabden close on my

heels. I wasn't shackled with chains or bound with ropes. I could have made a run for it, but I knew I wouldn't get very far. Father Ormskirk could easily ride me down, and half a dozen armed monks were immediately behind us – not to mention Brother Sabden, who needed only the smallest of excuses to hurt me.

I was leading them towards an abandoned farmhouse with a new occupant – the stone-chucker boggart. I'd chosen it because it was a familiar location, and as it was temporarily abandoned I also knew I wouldn't get anyone in trouble – though, I thought to myself, I had already got somebody in serious trouble. I'd betrayed Spook Johnson, and Tom Ward too. I had given the Quisitor all the evidence he needed to torture and burn them both.

I couldn't really pretend that I hadn't understood the consequences of my lies. I'd merely thrust it all to the back of my mind in order to save my skin. I'd tried to tell myself that it didn't matter, that the witch would already have killed them. But what if they did manage to get free? Death was still waiting for them. And the Quisitor would now use my lies as an excuse to execute spooks all over the County.

I was ashamed of myself. I'd done it because I was terrified of Brother Sabden and his instruments of torture. I felt like a coward, but I'd have done anything to escape such horrors.

As for the hope offered by the faceless demon, I'd done everything it had suggested. Now I was in the open air, away from the abbey, and I had to hope that the beast would come and save me, as promised. After that I would flee, go anywhere – so long as it was as far from Salford as possible.

I wondered about the demon. What if *this* time it had been lying? Even when tormenting me, it had always told the truth, but there was a first time for everything. That was another reason why I'd chosen the farm haunted by the boggart. If I wasn't rescued, it would be my last chance to escape. When we approached the farmhouse, the boggart was certain to attack. If I could get into the house alone, I might just be able to escape through the back door. It was a slim chance, but I was desperate – this was my final hope.

All too soon we came in sight of the farm. There was no sign of the demon's beast. I would have to help myself.

'Is that the farm we seek?' asked the Quisitor, pointing ahead impatiently.

'Yes, Father,' I replied, and we hastened towards it.

The farm was as I remembered it: just a two-storey house, with a small barn bordering a gated yard. The meadow was empty now. No doubt a neighbour was caring for the flock of sheep and the cow. As the animals had been moved, they must have retrieved the farmer's body as well.

I soon heard little pebbles falling around us, just as they had when I'd first approached the farmhouse. They sounded barely louder than drops of rain. Nobody around me seemed to have noticed, but I knew that the stones would soon get bigger and more dangerous.

They did. Now there were cries of pain behind me; one hit the Quisitor's horse and it reared up. He quickly brought it under control and glared down at me, demanding an explanation. I knew exactly what I was going to say.

'The cache of bone charms is guarded by a dangerous spirit,' I told him.

He looked at me askance. 'You never mentioned this before,' he said angrily.

'Well, it's better if I go in alone. I hope it will recognize me and allow me to approach the farmhouse. That way nobody will get hurt,' I pointed out.

'Then go ahead, Brother Beowulf. In case the evil spirit is in a less than generous mood, we will pray for your safety,' Father Ormskirk said, his voice heavy with sarcasm.

Before he could change his mind, I strode off, though I didn't break into a run. I was hoping that the door would open – I wouldn't have time to pray it open as I had on the previous occasion. I was very afraid. At any moment the boggart might hurl a stone that would smash my skull.

I opened the gate and began to cross the yard. I looked up at the roof, but I could see no sign of the creature. It had chosen to remain invisible.

I don't suppose it liked any human much – especially humans who dared to approach a building it had chosen as its abode. No doubt it had a strong dislike of quisitors too. In any case, he was an obvious and easy target, sitting high up on his big black horse.

However, I still didn't expect what happened next.

I'd almost reached the farmhouse door when I heard the sound of something heavy being heaved off the roof. I glanced back, and saw a boulder falling towards the Quisitor. It was even bigger than his head – and that's what it made contact with. I watched him fall backwards off his horse with a strangled cry, which was quickly silenced.

Nobody could have survived that blow.

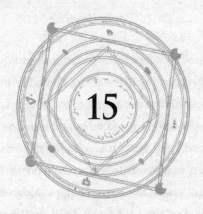

THE BEAST WITH
TWO HEADS

There was no time to waste. Grasping the door handle, I realized, with a sigh of relief, that there was no need to invoke St Quentin, the patron saint of locks: it yielded to my touch.

Then I was inside and running through the dusty, gloomy rooms, heading for the back door. It took me what seemed like an eternity to force it open. It wasn't locked – just swollen with damp, probably because of the recent heavy rain; there had been no fire in the house for days.

Outside that door there was an area of rough grass with a few trees, and then a slope leading down towards a narrow stream. I ran down and leaped across the stream, then kept running. By now I was out of sight of the monks. Even if Father Ormskirk wasn't dead – which seemed unlikely – he would surely be badly injured and they'd be preoccupied with helping their master.

But eventually, whatever the situation, they would certainly not be meekly returning to the abbey. Not with Brother Sabden in charge. Despite the danger from the boggart, they'd enter the house, find out I'd tricked them and hunt me down.

I had a head start, and I had to make the most of it.

I continued east towards some hills. At first I made good progress, but soon the steep slopes slowed me down considerably. The time I'd spent in the cell had weakened me. I was weary, and hungry too.

Late in the afternoon I saw that my fears had been realized. The monks were indeed following me. From the summit of a hill I saw a line of dark-clad men following my trail, their weapons glinting in the sun. There was no sign of either the horse or its rider. With a chill of fear, I realized that they must have used the animal to carry the Quisitor's body back to the abbey.

They would blame me for whatever had happened, and would seek revenge. I stared at the distant figures. The one in front seemed to be taller and thinner than the others. Without doubt it was Brother Sabden.

I turned and ran on as fast as I could.

The sun was just on the horizon when they caught their first glimpse of me. Once again, I was almost at the top of a hill. I heard shouts and saw them pointing at me. They set off again, picking up their pace.

I knew that my only chance was to keep ahead of them until dark. Then, if I still had the strength, I could change direction and perhaps escape them altogether. Once I'd reached the summit, I saw a wood below me. It gave me fresh hope, and I forced my legs to go faster, finally stumbling in among the trees just as my pursuers appeared on the hill behind me.

I kept going. I knew that they'd be able to follow me by the sound of twigs cracking beneath my boots, but I couldn't afford to slow down and walk more carefully, and it was hopeless to stop and try to hide yet. They would surely spread out behind me.

Then a voice I recognized called out behind me.

'I'll pull your teeth first – one by one!' Brother Sabden shouted. 'But I'll leave you your tongue and your eyes so that I can hear you scream and beg for mercy. I want you to see exactly what's being done to you after that. You led Father Ormskirk to his death – you're on the side of Hell, and that's for sure! There is only one punishment for that. You'll be hung, drawn and quartered before being cast, alive and in agony, onto fiery coals!'

I shivered in terror. What he was threatening was the most terrible death of all: a prolonged execution usually reserved for traitors or those who preached heresy. They hanged you until you choked and almost died. Then they cut you down, slit open your stomach and did terrible things to your insides. Finally, still alive, you were hanged again – though it seemed that Brother Sabden would prefer to end it by burning me. What's more, he would enjoy it.

I staggered on, my breath sobbing in my throat.

The wood was growing gloomier, yet the sun should still be above the horizon. Why was it getting dark so quickly? I wondered. Then I saw tendrils of mist wrapping themselves around my legs, undulating like lithe grey snakes.

I could still hear my pursuers, but now they seemed more distant. The mist was thickening. Then I heard something else . . .

Somewhere ahead of me I could hear thin, high, reedy notes. Someone was playing the pipes. There was something compelling about the sound. The music drew me on, and it never crossed my mind that I might be approaching danger.

I stumbled into a clearing and saw a fire, and beside it someone was sitting on a log looking at me.

It was the beast with two heads.

One head was much larger than the other. The smaller one had its eyes closed while the eyes of the first were wide and staring.

I shivered in fear. I felt that terrible cold which tells me I'm close to a ghost or something from Hell.

Then the larger head smiled and spoke to me – and in that instant everything changed.

Although for a moment it had looked like the beast foretold by the demon, it was really only a mother and child. The baby was bound to the mother's chest so that its head nestled at her throat.

The young woman was dressed in a green skirt and blouse, and a brown cape. Her long dark hair was tied up in a bun.

'Well. You must be Brother Beowulf. You look fit to drop. Come and sit next to me,' she invited. 'You must be hungry. Help yourself.'

It was then that I saw the two rabbits on spits over the fire and smelled their delicious aroma. As if in a dream, I approached and did as she'd suggested.

'You really *are* hungry!' she laughed as I lifted one of the spits, almost drooling as my teeth sank into the hot flesh, not caring if I burned my mouth. I began to eat ravenously.

Then I paused as I remembered Brother Sabden – hot on my heels only moments before. 'Wait! I'm being followed! The Quisitor's servants are after me! I'll be tortured and killed if they catch me!' I cried, turning round to listen. But the mist was now a thick grey curtain beyond the trees.

'Ain't nothing to worry about,' the young woman said. 'Father Ormskirk's dead – slain by that boggart. Just what he deserved. And as for the rest, by now they'll be befuddled and lost. They won't find us here.'

'How on earth do you know what happened to the Quisitor?' I asked, astonished.

She gave a sly grin, though it wasn't unfriendly. 'I'm Alice and I got my methods. Been watching you too. Got here as fast as I could.'

I looked at her in even greater astonishment. I was talking to the witch that Tom Ward lived with! But how could she have known all that? Had she been using magic to spy on me? I shivered as the cold ran up and down my spine. I was sitting on a log next to a really powerful witch. Our shoulders were almost touching. However, my hunger was too urgent to worry about that now. I carried on eating until there were only bones remaining.

'You finished? Had enough?' she asked, amused.

'Yes, thanks.'

'Good. Now it's my turn. While I'm eating, you can tell me what was in the letter from Tom.'

I gaped at her as she reached forward and lifted the second spit from the two forked sticks that held it above the fire. Then she began to eat, tearing off pieces of rabbit with her teeth. She ate more like a savage animal than a young woman – though it was exactly what I'd been doing, I reflected.

'Tell me what was in the letter!' she repeated, and this time there was a note of command in her voice.

I didn't even bother asking how she knew about it. More magic, no doubt.

'Tom wrote it just before he went to deal with the witch that had snatched Spook Johnson. He did it in case he didn't come back, and he asked me to take it to Chipenden and give it to you. Well, he didn't come back, and I was going to do as he said – but then the Quisitor arrived. He took me to the abbey and threatened to torture me—' I stopped, ashamed when I realized what I would have to admit to.

'I'm sorry, but I was terrified of the pain and I told them lies,' I said, blurting it all out. 'I told them what they wanted to hear. I said that spooks used magic spells and rituals. And that there was a cache of bone amulets in the house where the boggart was . . . and so that's why we were at the farmer's cottage.'

Alice frowned. 'Can't say I'm happy about what you said, but I know why you did it. And probably no harm's been done. Quisitor's dead, ain't he? And once I've taken care of Brother Sabden, there won't be a problem. But you certainly know how to try my patience, Brother Beowulf, because now I'm asking for the third time. *What did Tom write in that letter to me?*'

I blushed, and apologized. 'Firstly, he said he was really sorry for leaving you alone. He said his first duty was to be at your side when you had the baby. Then he said that you were not to come after him and try to help. He said you had a duty of your own, and that was to stay in Chipenden and protect your child.'

For a moment Alice didn't speak; she just stared into the fire. 'That's it? Is that all? Are you sure he didn't say anything else?' she asked insistently.

I paused. 'He said he loved you – that he would always love you.'

Alice nodded and gave a little smile.

'Well, by now Tom Ward should have learned a few things about me. He should know that when someone orders me to do something, I'm more than likely to do the exact opposite. So here I am, despite my master's instructions,' Alice said with a smile, her voice full of mockery, 'and with a little help from you, Brother Beowulf, I'm sure we can sort things out. I know a lot of what's happened, but I'd like you to tell me everything, right from the beginning. Could you do that, please?' she said, and, although she was still smiling, her voice was very firm.

So I told her almost everything. I missed out the visitations by the faceless demon. I couldn't bear to tell anyone about that. Tom already knew that I saw ghosts – that was bad enough – but no one would want to know me if they thought I was in the power of a demon . . .

When I'd finished my tale, Alice thanked me and then grew very serious.

'Tomorrow we'll go and take a look at that village,' she told me. 'Now I need some privacy, so move yourself to the other side of the fire and get some sleep. You'll be needing all your strength in the morning!'

I did as she said. I was exhausted. First I glanced back across the fire and saw that the baby no longer nestled at her throat. She was feeding it.

Then, despite the hard, damp ground and my throbbing forehead, I had barely closed my eyes before I was sound asleep.

Alice woke me. Her fingers were holding my fringe away from my forehead, and she was pressing something cold and wet against the brand.

'You told me they threatened torture, but you didn't say they'd actually branded you. That should help with the pain. Can't do much about the mark, but your hair should hide it.'

I sat up and reached out towards my forehead, but she seized me by the wrist and pulled my hand away. 'It's just a herb. It'll fall off once it has dried out. Let it do its work.'

'I thought you knew everything that had happened to me?' I said to her.

Alice shook her head. 'Couldn't be watching all the time, could I? But I'm sorry. Because you're so young, I didn't think they'd actually torture you. And I got here as soon as I could.'

She went round to the other side of the embers and came back holding something. It was a hard-boiled egg, which she slipped into my hand. As she did so, she kept half an eye on her baby, who was lying peacefully on the other side of the fire, making small snuffling noises.

'Sorry, Brother Beowulf, but that's all the breakfast we have time for,' she said. 'Maybe we can eat properly later.

Your name's a bit of a mouthful, isn't it? Would you mind if I just called you Beowulf?'

'Not at all,' I told her. 'If you'd like my name even shorter, just call me Wulf. That's what Tom did.'

'Yes – Wulf – I like that. Do you know what a *true name* is?' she asked.

I shook my head.

'Well, it ain't necessarily the name everybody calls you by – though sometimes it can be. A true name's one that says who you really are, and I think Wulf might well be your true name!' Then she laughed. 'Never tell a witch your true name or you'll be in her power for ever! But it's a bit late for that now, ain't it, Wulf!'

If she was making a joke of it, it was a scary one, and it made me feel uneasy.

'What kind of a witch are you?' I blurted out. She didn't look like someone who would drink blood or cut off thumbs, but appearances could be deceptive.

'I'm not the kind of witch that Spook Johnson will have heard about. As far as I know, I'm the only one of my kind. I'm an earth witch and I serve the god Pan.'

'Have you ever seen him?' I asked.

'Of course I have. He's never very far away. Leaves are his eyes and twigs are his fingers. Didn't you hear him playing his pipes? That's what drew you here.'

Yes, I had heard the music, but I had assumed it was Alice playing. I felt uneasy. Pan was a pagan god, and he almost certainly had his own place in Hell. How had I become so close to such devilish forces?

I was still hungry as I followed Alice westwards. She was carrying the baby strapped to her chest, and I took the large battered leather bag she'd given me. It was similar to the one used by Tom Ward. I wondered if it was his old one. It was certainly heavy.

Soon we were approaching the village where the witch lived. Alice was still in the lead, as if she knew the way better than I did. The sky was grey and there was a slight chill in the air, and I looked through the trees nervously. What if Brother Sabden and his armed monks were still around?

'Don't worry about that Brother Sabden,' said Alice, as if reading my mind. 'He's gone back to the abbey. Probably won't come looking for you again until they've buried the Quisitor. Anyway, we've got more important things to worry about, we have.'

We arrived at the village just before the sun set. From the hill it looked the same as ever. Alice frowned, sniffed loudly three times and shook her head. 'It's worse than I thought,' she said. 'But there's no immediate danger.'

She led the way down the hill without bothering to stay among the trees, then crossed the street and went straight to the shop. Inside there was the smell of wood rot. The ceiling had fallen in, and plaster lay on the wet floor. The food for sale had gone. The shop seemed as if it had been abandoned for years.

After a quick look, Alice beckoned me back outside.

'Last time you were here, it wasn't like this, was it?' she asked me.

'It was very different,' I replied. 'The shop was stocked with food – and there was a little girl of three or maybe four. She took me down the street and I looked through a window and saw the witch. Now it's all a ruin. It looks like the whole village has been abandoned and deserted for years!'

Alice nodded. 'Things ain't what they seem,' she said. 'I need to take a good look around and see what's what. Would you mind holding my daughter?'

She held the baby out towards me. 'Make a cradle with your arms, Wulf – that's it. She won't break and she won't bite – at least not until she gets her first teeth. Her name is Tilda, but I call her Tilda the Terrible! And you'll know why I gave her that title if she wakes up and starts to cry!'

Nervously, I took the baby in my arms. I'd been the youngest in my family and had never held such a tiny baby before. I was scared of dropping her, but Alice made me sit down on the step where I could support my arms with my knees, and I began to feel easier about it. Tilda was sleeping peacefully – she didn't look so terrible to me . . .

Alice left me there and began to walk away along the street. She peered through each window, and at one point closed her eyes and put her forehead against a closed door, resting it there for quite a while.

As she was doing this, the baby woke up and began to cry. Then howl. Then scream. I realized that Alice had named her well. Tilda was in a terrible rage. She was screaming fit to wake the dead and her face was almost purple.

Alice quickly came back and took her from me. Tilda quietened almost immediately. I studied Alice's face as she held her baby. She kissed Tilda on the forehead with great tenderness and whispered into her ears. I could see an expression of intense love on her face as she gazed down at her baby. If this young woman was a witch, she was also first and foremost a loving and protective mother.

Her attention was focused on her daughter at the moment, but I suspected that Tom would not be far from Alice's thoughts. How awful it was for her to be aware that she might never see him again, that Tom might never gaze upon his daughter as she was doing now.

Alice turned to me. 'Let's go back up the hill, Wulf – I've seen enough.'

I followed her up to the summit, where we found somewhere with a good view of the village below us, and sat down. By now the sun had set and shadows were gathering. Down in the village it had grown very dark.

'Now, Wulf, I need you to do something for me,' Alice said, and I could tell from her tone that I wasn't going to like it. 'It's dangerous, and you'll have to leave this world to do it. Don't like to ask you but I ain't got no choice. You've seen how this child depends on me. I could maybe go myself and leave her behind with you, Wulf, but if something happened to me you might not be able to protect her and you certainly couldn't feed her. And I daren't risk taking her with me either. Don't like to do it, but I'm asking you to go.'

'Leave this world and go where?' I asked in terror. 'You mean go into Hell?'

'We don't call it Hell,' said Alice; 'we call it the dark.'

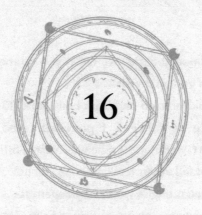

16

EXEUNT

Alice gave me a little smile. 'I ain't actually asking you to go into the dark,' she explained. 'You see, there are places hidden from this world, inhabited by things that are invisible to humans. Some folks call 'em "underworlds". The Hollow Hills is one of them, and that's in Ireland. There are lots of others. Powerful things from the dark can create their own refuges. They're hidden from our world, yet close to it. It makes it easy for them to prey on people here. That's where Johnson and Tom are being held – I'm sure of it.'

'What would this hidden place be like?' I asked her nervously.

'You've been there already, Wulf, when you walked into the village shop and talked to that strange child – and when you looked through the window at the sleeping witch,' she told me. 'That explains why it looked like a shop, while now it's just abandoned ruins. So, when you go there, it'll look like it did on your last visit.'

'But Spook Johnson and Tom both failed to come back! What chance do *I* have?' I protested. 'And look what happened to Gwen Raddle. She was blasted into tiny pieces and her head fell at our feet!'

'I ain't pretending it won't be dangerous, Wulf, but this time you'll have me to give you some help. Can't come with you, but I'm an earth witch, and I can give you things to take with you that might help—'

'*Might help!*' I interrupted. 'That's not much good! You're saying that you can't guarantee that I'll be safe.'

'Witches don't blast people into pieces. Witches don't usually live in an underworld either. Whatever this entity is, it's different, so nobody can guarantee you'll be safe. We're dealing with something that's unknown; something very powerful. I know there's a risk, but I have to ask you to do it. Think of it this way: it'll make up for the other things you've done . . .'

It was the first time Alice had tried to make me feel bad, and the shock must have shown on my face. Still, I couldn't blame her for putting pressure on me. She was just doing her best to get Tom back – but she looked stricken, all the same.

'Oh! I'm sorry, Wulf, I shouldn't have said that . . .' she murmured.

'No, you had every right to say it. I'll go,' I told her.

She was right. Despite the danger, I had to go. I'd betrayed both spooks. I had to make up for that or I wouldn't be able to live with myself. Alice had rescued me from torture and death. I owed her for that too. She had good reasons for not going. I had to do it.

'You mean it?' she asked.

'Yes.'

She gave me a really warm smile. Her whole face lit up, and I saw how pretty she was. I could understand why Tom Ward liked her.

'Thanks, Wulf,' she said, rummaging around in her bag. When she stood up, she was holding a few small items in her left hand. One of them was a key.

'I'm sorry I can't help you more,' Alice continued. 'You see, I ain't been the same since I first knew that Tilda was growing inside me. My magic used to be really powerful, but now it's just a shadow of what it once was. These should be enough to improve your chances. The first one isn't magical, though – it's a key. Take it . . .'

I accepted the key and examined it closely. It wasn't rusty, but there was nothing special about it.

'Old Gregory, the spook who trained Tom, had a brother who was a master locksmith. He made a couple of special keys that would open almost any lock. Tom has one, and this is its twin. That's another thing that worries me. If that witch has locked Tom up somewhere, he should be able to use his key to escape. But he ain't escaped . . . Still, if you do find Tom and Johnson and they're locked away, at least you'll be able to free them.'

I put the key in my trouser pocket and looked back at Alice, who was holding a second item out towards me. I shivered, and the hair on the back of my neck began to rise. It looked like a couple of small magpie feathers bound together by a twist of bark and grass. I could sense the dark magic radiating from it and was reluctant to even touch it.

'Take it,' Alice said, thrusting it at me firmly. 'You may well need it. It's called *exeunt* and is a spell of undoing. It ain't too far removed in what it does from the special key I gave you. It opens a door. Sometimes an underworld won't release those who enter it. So just separate those feathers and, in an instant, you'll be back in this world. But if you find Tom and Johnson, you need to be touching them so they can come back with you. Understand?'

I nodded. Those feathers would be our only way to escape the witch.

'Here's something else, Wulf,' Alice went on, handing me a dagger. 'It belonged to one of the spooks who lived in Chipenden long before Tom began his apprenticeship there. The blade is made of a silver alloy and is deadly to creatures of the dark.'

I accepted it with a nod and put it in my pocket, even though I couldn't imagine myself stabbing anyone.

'If I do manage to bring Tom and Spook Johnson back with me, what happens when the witch follows us?' I asked. 'You said your magic wasn't powerful any more, and we know that she's really dangerous.'

Alice shook her head, but she looked determined. 'My magic might not be what it once was, but I ain't completely helpless. Still someone to be reckoned with, I am, especially when I've got this child to protect. So don't you worry about that, Wulf. Just get Tom and Johnson back here and I'll do the rest.'

I began to walk down the hill into the gloom. Suddenly I thought of something that puzzled me, and I halted, turning back to Alice.

'How do you know that the underworld will be there when I reach the bottom of the hill?' I asked.

'Each underworld has defences, Wulf, and it sensed what I was. Sometimes it tries to keep out other witches or any kind of serious threat just by hiding – which was why it looked abandoned just now. It didn't see Gwen Raddle as dangerous; that's why it let her in. It won't see you as a threat either. It didn't even see Tom or Johnson as threatening. It'll be there waiting for you this time – trust me.'

I nodded, turned and continued down the hill. I was afraid, and had to force myself to keep walking, doing my best not to think about what had happened to Gwen Raddle. I left the trees, crossed the road and approached the shop. Already I could sense that it was no longer deserted.

There were candles flickering inside.

I had entered the underworld of the witch.

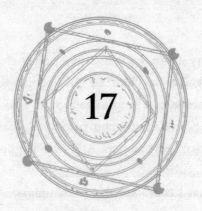

17

THE MEAT SAFE

The shop was no longer derelict. As before, the shelves were laden with packets and bags – there were herbs, medicines, sugar and salt . . . Pots and pans gleamed brightly on their hooks, and on the floor lay overflowing sacks of vegetables.

The same child, the little girl with flaming red hair and green eyes, turned to look at me. This time she was seated on a high stool at the counter and was drawing with a pencil.

'What do you want, priest? You shouldn't have come back!' she said, scowling at me.

'I came to see you. What are you drawing?' I asked with a smile, trying to be as friendly as possible. All the while my heart was thumping with fear. There was terrible danger here.

'I'm making a storybook!' she declared.

'What's it about?'

'It's a story about a witch with a pointy chin and a big wart on the end of her chin. She gives people hegets.'

'Why does she give people headaches?' I asked.

'The hegets aren't important, priest. It's what she does to their heads that really matters. And what she does gives 'em bad hegets.'

Once again I could see that, although she looked very young, this was no ordinary child: she was far older than her appearance suggested. I moved closer to the counter, the better to see what she was drawing.

'That's really good,' I told her. 'Just like the witch you showed me last time.'

It was an excellent sketch, an exact replica of what I'd seen. The witch was in profile, and her face was shaped like the crescent moon, her chin and forehead its horns.

'Do you want me to take you to see her – like last time?' she asked.

I hesitated. I needed to choose my words carefully. 'Maybe you could do that later, but I'm really looking for two friends of mine . . .'

'What are their names, priest?' the girl wanted to know.

'One's called Will Johnson and the other's Tom Ward.'

She gave me a smile. It wasn't very friendly. There was something sly about it.

'Names are important,' she said. 'Johnson is the big fat man, isn't he? Ward is younger.'

'Yes, that's right. Do you know where they are?' I asked her.

'Perhaps I do, and perhaps I could take you there, but first you must tell me *your* name.'

There was something calculating in her eyes when she said that, and I suddenly remembered what Alice had told me – that a witch could gain power over you if she knew your true name. With a sinking feeling in my stomach, I realized that I'd just put my big foot in it again. I might have given her the true names of both spooks. Perhaps she hadn't known them – particularly Tom's – until I'd blurted them out. It was too late to do anything about that, but Wulf was my true name and I wasn't going to tell her that.

'My name is Brother Beowulf,' I told her. 'Could you please take me to see my two friends?'

By way of reply, the child climbed down from the stool. She came past me, opened the shop door and stepped outside. I followed her as she crossed the street and began to climb the hill towards the trees where I'd left Alice.

Soon we were in the wood, and I was worried that we might actually come across Alice and her baby, but there was no sign of them. Although everything looked similar, this was one of the underworlds, I reminded myself. I was now in the magical lair of some malignant witch.

Without glancing back at me, the child headed south in the direction of Salford. I couldn't believe that this world was so large. It was like another version of the one I lived in.

However, looking up, I realized that there was something strange about the sky; something I'd noticed last time: a red glow. Last time I was here there had been clouds, but now, although the heavens were clear, I could see no stars – just an empty red sky.

Heavens! I'd used the wrong word. Above me was not heaven. Whatever Alice called this place, I was surely in one of the infernal regions.

This underworld was just an extension of Hell, and it threatened those who entered it on every side.

As we walked along the main street of Salford, all the houses were in darkness. Apart from our footsteps everything was strangely quiet. It was weird and disturbing. Did anyone dwell in those houses? I wondered. If so, they would certainly not be alive.

At last we stood before Spook Johnson's house – or at least the version of it to be found in this underworld. There were no lights showing in the windows. The child placed her small hand against the door and pushed until it swung back on its hinges. Nervously I followed her into the gloom.

'Down there!' she said, pointing to the stairs that led to the cellar. 'That's where your friends are, priest.'

That was where Spook Johnson imprisoned his witches in the real world. A single torch was all that illuminated that grim place.

I knew what I would find even before I reached the foot of the stairs, and I was proved correct. There were no witches in the cells here.

'There are your friends!' crowed the strange child, following me down.

Spook Johnson and Tom Ward were in separate cells. Both lay on their backs on the flagged floor, either dead or unconscious. I moved closer to the bars and peered in at each in turn. To my relief, I could see their chests rising and falling.

I called out to Tom Ward – 'Tom! Tom! Wake up! Wake up!' – but there was no reply. This was no natural sleep.

I tried to rouse Spook Johnson, but he didn't respond either, and he wasn't snoring. When asleep, he usually snored until the walls of the house shook and the slates rattled on the roof. I suspected that the spooks had either been drugged or subjected to dark magic.

Then I remembered the key that Alice had given to me. If I could get inside their cells and rouse them, then we could use the feathers to make our escape. There was no guard present – just the little girl.

'I don't like my friends being locked up like that,' I told her, reaching into my pocket for the special key.

Thankfully I didn't pull it out, for just then I was startled by the sudden sound of heavy boots thumping down the stairs towards us. I turned, and was horrified to see a huge figure thrusting its way with difficulty into the cellar.

It was a man-shaped creature with a large head covered with unruly hair, the fringe almost obscuring the eyes. If this *was* a man, I had never seen one so big and muscular. This was truly a giant. He was dressed in a rough leather jerkin and brown hemp trousers, and on his feet were enormous hobnailed boots. He was twice as broad as a normal man, with a neck like a bull, and so tall that he had to bow his head to avoid banging it on the ceiling.

He stared at me, and saliva trickled out of his mouth and down his chin.

'I think you'd be safer in a cell, priest,' the little girl said. 'It's quite a while since Grum had his lunch and he's ready for supper now. He thinks you look quite tasty.'

The man-beast opened his mouth and roared, the noise so loud and the breath so foul that I flinched and took a couple of nervous steps backwards. I did as the child suggested. I opened the door of the nearest cell and stepped inside.

As if by magic, the child produced a key from her left hand, inserted it in the lock and twisted it. There was a click, and I was locked inside. She smiled as if she'd done something really clever. I certainly seemed to have stepped into her trap – but I wasn't worried. I still had the key Alice had given me. Once the child and the giant had gone, we could escape.

'Now you're in a meat safe too, priest,' said the child.

She walked up to the giant and gripped two of his huge fingers with her left hand. The creature looked down at her but made no sound; there was a bewildered expression on his face. Then she led him up the cellar steps, and they both disappeared from view.

I knew that a meat safe was usually a cold store where meat was kept until it was time to cook it. I shuddered. Did they intend to eat us? I wondered in horror.

I decided to wait a few minutes in case they returned – but I couldn't wait for long. The cellar was only lit by a single torch and it was burning low. Soon we'd be plunged in darkness.

For the second time I reached into my pocket for the key. But once again I didn't get a chance to withdraw it because there was suddenly another noise on the stone steps – the sound of scratching – and it was getting louder. Something was approaching the cellar.

When the thing reached the bottom step, I couldn't at first make sense of what I was seeing. It appeared to be a very large spider, and it was now scuttling across the floor towards my cell. I stepped backwards in alarm, my heart in my mouth, because, although the creature wasn't large, I could sense the malevolence radiating from it. Now I was truly terrified.

The flickering torch was distorting what I was trying to see; it was hard to be sure where the creature ended and its dark shadow began. It was certainly very large – about the size of a rat – but it looked more like a spider: a small oval head atop a body supported by five triple-jointed legs. In addition it had a hooked nose that resembled an eagle's beak, pointy ears and a wide mouth. The face was rough and covered with what looked like purple pimples, while the body had green scales like those of a lizard. I noticed that one leg differed from the other four, consisting of bare black bone, serrated like the sharp teeth of a saw.

There was something loathsome and threatening about the creature – something deadly – and it was small enough to fit through the bars of my cell.

All at once it spoke to me, its voice hoarse and deep.

'You're a runt! You're far too small for me!'

How could a thing that size possess such a voice? I wondered. I could feel my legs trembling in terror, but I almost laughed. There was something ridiculous about such a small creature calling me a runt.

'But those two will do fine,' the spider continued. 'Especially the fat one. I think we'll use him first. Plenty of room there!'

It scuttled towards the steps and, in a voice deeper and louder than ever, called out: 'Grum! Grum! Down you come! It's time to get busy!'

The sound of big boots ponderously descending the stairs told me that the giant was on his way back. He lumbered into the cellar and, without glancing at me, thrust a key into the lock of Spook Johnson's cell. The key looked very tiny in his huge hand, but he managed to unlock the door and he dragged Johnson out. Then he did the same for Tom Ward.

I watched helplessly as the giant threw Johnson over one shoulder as if he were no heavier than a child. Then he carried him up the steps. Moments later he came down again to collect Tom Ward. He went back up with the hideous little creature scuttling up the stone steps at his heels.

No sound came from above. I waited for a while just in case they came back for me, but then I took the key from my pocket and inserted it into the lock. Would it work as Alice had promised? I wondered.

I should never have doubted her. The key turned smoothly, and then I was out of the cell.

My first plan was no longer possible. I saw that things would be more difficult than I had hoped, but somehow I had to reach the two spooks and use the feather spell to get all three of us to safety. I needed to follow the giant and see where he was taking them.

As I walked up the stairs, the torch flickered out behind me, so that the cellar was in total darkness. I emerged into an empty kitchen. Once more I listened. There was only silence. The big house was empty.

Cautiously I stepped outside. In the distance I could see the giant striding away along the deserted street with a spook over each shoulder. At his side scuttled the big spider. They were heading back towards the village.

So, keeping my distance, I followed them.

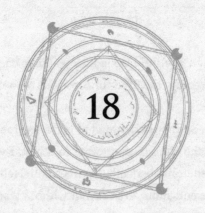

THE DEAD GIANT

As I left Salford, the sky continued to glow red, and there were plenty of shadows to hide me. I made good use of them, and crept along the side of the road, out of sight of Grum and the other creature.

I looked up at the sky again and realized that its red colour was exactly the same shade as the little girl's hair. That was strange, and I wondered if it was a coincidence or something more. I also wondered where she was now. Up to no good, I thought.

Eventually we came to the village again, but instead of continuing towards the grocer's shop, as I'd expected, the creatures halted outside the church. It had big double oak doors, large enough to get a farm cart and horses through, but there was a smaller one set within it. I heard a key turning in a lock, and then the giant opened it. He had difficulty fitting through the little door but, walking backwards, he managed to drag the two unconscious spooks into the church.

Once the spider had crawled in after him, I slowly approached the church, then came to a halt. I waited for a while in the shadows beneath the eaves until I felt reasonably sure they weren't about to come out without warning. What business did they have in a church? What were they going to do to the two spooks?

Again that chilling term 'meat safe' came back to me. I shuddered, then carefully opened the smaller door and crept inside. The church looked much like any other in a village of this size. There was just one stained-glass window above the altar; the others were made of thick, cheap clear glass. The wooden pews were old, in need of varnish, and a threadbare grey carpet led between them to the altar. The flickering light from a couple of candles near the fount was the only illumination.

Luckily I seemed to be alone. But where were the two creatures, along with their prey?

I noticed that the back of the altar was high – at least eight feet tall – and suddenly I had an idea. I knew there would be a crypt somewhere below the church, and it would almost certainly be reached from behind that altar. I felt sure that was where the spooks had been taken. I walked down the aisle slowly, listening for danger. Out of force of habit from my months at the abbey, I genuflected in front of the altar, then moved to the side and peered behind it.

I was right. An open trapdoor gave access to stone steps leading down. I began a careful descent, my heart hammering in my chest.

At the foot of the steps I found myself in the huge crypt. Normally such a place would have had the dry, dusty odour of long-dead bones, but this one smelled like an abattoir. The metallic reek of blood was heavy upon the air. About a dozen large stone coffins were stacked up against one wall of the crypt, but these weren't the source of the smell. Each was furnished with a heavy stone lid; each was sealed with lead. The foul odour of blood came from things piled on the shelves lining the other walls, stretching from the floor right up to the high ceiling. They were stacks of bones – human bones, which was only to be expected; this was a crypt, after all. Some were old and dry. That was also expected. But others were more recent additions. Some were still wet with blood.

I retched, and tried not to look. Were they cannibals, this witch and the giant? It was certainly beginning to look that way.

I carefully inched my way towards the far wall of the crypt, trying to make as little noise as possible. I couldn't see anyone, but I knew they must be nearby. Then, in front of me, I saw another trapdoor – also open. I peered down and saw a torch on a wall bracket at the foot of more steps.

I frowned. This was very unusual. In the County, even a small church might have a modest crypt to house the bones of the dead – mostly those of the more well-to-do families who could afford a large donation. But to have a level below that . . . what could be its purpose?

I reminded myself that this was not the world I had been born into. As Alice had told me, this was an underworld. Although it might look like mine, different rules applied, and they would be designed to help the witch who ruled this devilish realm.

To go down the new steps was a huge risk, and I was scared. I knew I might meet the giant and his accomplice coming back up. However, the spooks must be down there. I'd come this far; I couldn't abandon them now. So I began my descent.

At the bottom there was a tunnel leading off into a distant dark. The floor, walls and ceiling were made of hard-packed earth. I could see no wooden props or overhead beams to support the ceiling, so what was holding it up? I wondered. I sensed the great weight of soil and rock above me, but steeled myself to my task, and walked on.

The further I went from the steps and the flickering torch, the darker it became. But then the tunnel curved to the left and I could see light ahead – from another torch, positioned at the point where the single tunnel divided into two.

I faced another problem. Which one should I take? As far as I knew, there was no pathfinder saint, so I muttered a quick prayer for guidance to St Anthony, the patron saint of lost things and lost causes. I'd prayed to that saint before, and sometimes he'd helped me. This proved to be the case again.

St Anthony was never visible to me, but his croaky voice whispered into my right ear. It was a voice that quavered with age:

'Do not take the left-hand path of darkness. Keep always to the right!'

I did as he advised, and took the right-hand tunnel.

I wondered how far these tunnels extended. By now, I was surely well outside the boundary of the church and its grounds. There was another torch ahead, and once again the tunnel divided in two. I didn't bother with a prayer this time – St Anthony had told me to 'keep always to the right', and I was only too happy to follow the saint's guidance in this hellish place.

I went down the right-hand tunnel without hesitation. In fact, I was starting to walk faster. This was beginning to seem like a labyrinth, and there was a danger I might get lost. I hoped that, by taking the same fork each time on the way out, it would be easier to retrace my steps.

When I rounded the next corner, I noticed an open door to my left, a light shining from inside, and moved forward very slowly. This had to be the place. When I was almost at the door, I came to a halt and listened carefully. After a few minutes I was confident that there were no sounds coming from the other side, so I pushed it fully open and stepped into the room.

The first thing I noticed was the smell of fresh blood. The second was the figure sitting on a chair. It was the giant, and he was dead.

He'd been murdered. Someone had opened the top of his skull as if they were slicing off the top of an egg. Bile rising in my throat, I took a step nearer and saw that the skull was empty. Something had scooped out his brains. Despite this his face looked peaceful. His eyes were closed and his mouth was slack and open. No doubt he had been taken by surprise, his killer striking so swiftly that he'd had no time to feel fear or pain.

I backed away in panic. If something could do that to a giant, it could deal with me very easily. I considered my escape. I could leave the room and go back the way I'd come. Or I could use the feathers now, and escape this underworld. But then I thought of Tom Ward – Tom, who had always been kind to me. It was the memory of Tom rather than Johnson that halted me in my tracks.

And then there was my duty to Alice. How could I face her and admit that I had abandoned Tom?

So, very reluctantly, I checked the room for clues (making sure to avert my eyes from the murdered giant). Finding none – apart from drops of blood on a table, and a large empty bowl beside them – I returned to the tunnel and began to advance again.

Soon there was another branching of the tunnels, so again I selected the right-hand option. Immediately there was another open door to the left, again with light flickering from within. Was this where the two spooks were being held? I wondered.

Cautiously I crept forward, keeping out of sight as much as possible. I could hear what sounded like sucking and sipping noises. Someone or something was inside the room.

I peered in through the door – and saw three of the strange spider-like creatures feeding at a shallow wooden tray on the ground. It was full of dark blood and small pieces of meat.

For a moment I wasn't sure what I was seeing ... and then, in a moment of horrified realization, my mind flashed back to the open skull of the giant, and suddenly I knew what the creatures were. I had read about them in Spook Johnson's library. They were a type of witch's familiar from the highest and most deadly category of all: one of the most terrifying creatures that came from what Alice called the 'dark', but which I could see all too clearly was really Hell.

They were called 'brain guzzlers'.

THE HIERARCHY OF FAMILIARS

I knew that not all witches used familiars – some preferred blood or bone magic. In fact, as Johnson had explained, spooks placed witches in three main categories according to the type of magic they used. There were bone witches, blood witches and familiar witches.

A familiar was a creature that served a witch. She would make a cut on her upper arm and let it feed on her blood. Eventually a small nipple would grow on her flesh, making the feeding much easier. In exchange for the blood of its mistress, the familiar served her by spying, or even killing her enemies. Poisonous toads, rats, crows and cats were common familiars, but the brain guzzlers feeding from the tray were a different thing altogether. They were right at the very top of the hierarchy of Hell's familiars. They were born there.

I now recognized the fifth appendage I'd seen on the spider-creature – the one with the serrated edge. The book I'd read explained that the witch would send her chosen victim into a deep sleep, and then the creature would use its leg as a saw to slice through the top of the skull, exposing the brain, which it would then devour, taking up residence inside the skull. I realized that the giant must be such a victim. He was not dead, but he no longer had a mind or will of his own. He only came 'alive' when the familiar was in his head. It was a type of possession.

I watched the creatures drinking from the tray. Maybe the witch's blood couldn't provide enough food for so many familiars, so it had to be supplemented in this way?

I remembered what the ugly little creature had said:

You're a runt! You're far too small for me!

Then, indicating Tom Ward and Spook Johnson, it had added, *But those two will do fine.*

Was that what had happened here? The larger victims such as the giant were possessed, while the smaller, unsuitable ones such as me became food? Or were these foul beasts feasting on one of the spooks?

I had to act quickly. There were three familiars here, but there might well be others close by. Somewhere in this maze they might even now be sawing into the skulls of the two spooks and devouring their contents.

I crept away, trying my best not to make a noise. I needn't have worried. The three familiars were still too busy slurping down the grisly contents of their tray to notice me. I continued onwards until I reached the next fork in the tunnel, and once more chose the right-hand path. The tunnels seemed to go on for ever. Perhaps they did. In this construct of dark magic, anything was possible.

Once again I saw a door on the left and heard sounds coming from the room behind it – terrible sounds that set my teeth on edge. It was the sound of sawing.

Knowing it could only mean one thing, I crept in.

I was right: the scene before me looked like something out of a butcher's shop. Tom Ward and Spook Johnson were tightly bound to chairs. Johnson's was right next to a table, and one of the weird little familiars was crouching on the tabletop, about to saw into the spook's head with its little bone-saw.

Tom Ward was still unconscious, but to my horror I saw that Johnson's eyes were open and his mouth was working frantically as if he were trying to speak; instead he was just making little whimpering sounds. Then he looked at me and his eyes widened. Despite what was being done to him, he seemed to know who I was.

As the familiar sawed into his head, blood flowed from the wound and ran down his face. It was a desperate situation, and desperate measures were called for. I acted without thought, drawing the silver-alloy dagger from my pocket. I lunged forward, and stabbed downwards fast and hard, pushing the creature away from Johnson's head and pinning it to the tabletop.

It shrieked in agony, but that cry didn't last long because I stabbed it again and again until it gave a final twitch and fell silent.

Then, with trembling hands, I used the blade to cut Spook Johnson free. It wasn't easy. As I did so, I glanced at his head. There was so much blood that it was hard to see how much damage had been done. I knew head wounds always bled a lot, though; hopefully it was only shallow.

Once free, Johnson staggered to his feet, groaning and touching his palm gingerly to his bleeding head. He then put a heavy hand on my shoulder, as if seeking support, and limped after me as I went to free Tom.

I'd just finished cutting through the ropes that bound him when I heard steps approaching. We'd been discovered! The witch must have sensed that we were deep within her lair, and now her face slid into view in the doorway. It was like a horned moon drifting towards us out of the darkness. I knew I had to get us out *now*.

Johnson already had his hand on my shoulder to support himself. So I leaned forward, gripping Tom's arm with my right hand so that all three of us were in contact, as Alice had instructed. I reached into my pocket with my left hand to separate the two feathers and activate the spell.

Out of the corner of my eye, I could see the witch filling the doorway, glaring at us malevolently, raising her clawed hand. Just as I separated the feathers, there was a flash of light and a force that threw me backwards.

I thought it was just the effects of Alice's spell, but when I opened my eyes I was on my knees in the street outside the church. The red glow was gone from the sky; overhead the stars were dim but visible. The brightening to the east told me that it was almost dawn. We'd escaped from the underworld – I could have wept with relief.

I looked about me and saw that Johnson was on his knees too, dazed, and still bleeding badly from the head wound. However, to my dismay there was no sign of Tom Ward. The blast from the witch must have thrown us apart, breaking the contact. He was still in her clutches.

We staggered to our feet, crossed the street and silently began to climb the hill towards the trees. Alice walked down to meet us with her baby.

I will never forget the terrible look of anguish in her eyes when she saw that Tom wasn't with us.

As we headed back into the trees, I explained what had happened. Alice listened in silence, and then gave me Tilda to hold while she tended to Spook Johnson.

She bathed his cut and then took leaves out of a pouch and bound them to the wound with strips of cloth that she'd cut from his shirtsleeves. As she worked, tears ran down her cheeks. They were for Tom. No doubt she believed that she'd lost him for ever. I shuddered at the thought, though it seemed likely, and so I had no words of hope for her. By now another of the familiars might well be sawing into his skull. I tried not to think about it.

'I'll go back into the underworld,' I offered. 'Could you make another spell so that I can get us both out? Have you enough magic left for that?'

She nodded, still silently weeping, and I handed her the two feathers. Alice sat down cross-legged on the grass, facing me. I glanced at Spook Johnson. He was staring at us both, his gaze quickly flicking from one to the other, but he didn't speak. I wondered if the wicked little familiar had actually cut deep enough into his skull to damage his brain.

'Those brain guzzlers are dangerous,' Alice said, almost as though she'd read my mind. 'I should know. Bony Lizzie, the witch who trained me, had one as her familiar. Nasty little thing it was. We didn't get on. We both knew one of us was going to die eventually, so I killed it before it could kill me.'

There was something chilling about the calm way she said it. But how could I blame her? I'd just killed a guzzler to save Spook Johnson.

'There's something else, Wulf. I told you that my magic faded away as soon as I felt Tilda kick inside me,' Alice said, and I nodded, remembering. 'But since she was born it's started to come back. I'm getting stronger by the day. And if that witch has harmed Tom, I'll go in there and sort her, then kill every single one of her familiars. That ain't no empty threat either. I'll make her curse the day she was born!'

She said this so fiercely, I couldn't doubt her.

'I'll go back now!' I said, coming to my feet, aware that every second that passed reduced the chance of Tom being alive.

Alice gestured for me to sit down and shook her head. 'I can do the spell to get you out, Wulf, but you won't be able to enter that underworld until night falls again. That's just the way things are. Need to wait till then.'

I almost blurted out that nightfall would be too late for Tom, but I bit my lip. Alice knew the situation. There was no need to say anything.

Suddenly Johnson gave a spluttering cough and started to speak. His voice was hoarse and his speech uneven.

'You must be Alice,' he said. 'Me and Tom were imprisoned together for a long time and he mostly talked about you. He said he'd forbidden you to try and help him, but that you'd probably ignore him.'

'He knows me so well,' Alice said with a bitter smile.

Johnson suddenly frowned. 'He also told me that you were a witch, but I had to learn that not all witches were evil. To be honest, I find that very hard to accept. But you helped this boy get me out of that hell-hole, so for now I'll make a special effort to push it to the back of my mind.'

'Yes, I'd do that if I was you,' said Alice, smiling sweetly but with an edge of sarcasm to her voice. 'You should try really hard to follow Tom's advice.'

'I'll do more than just follow his advice, girl. At nightfall I'll go back into that underworld with the boy and we'll bring Tom safely back.'

Alice didn't say anything, just gave Johnson the slightest of nods, but the tears started to trickle down her cheeks again. I felt a lump in my throat. We both knew that she was unlikely to see Tom again.

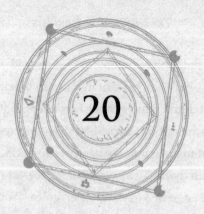

20

THE DANCING BEAR

We headed north for about a mile to put some distance between us and the village, and settled down in a clearing in a wood.

I got to hold Tilda again while Alice went hunting for rabbits. I would have offered, but I hadn't a clue how to catch them. Spook Johnson didn't offer either: by then he was lying on his back under a tree, snoring loud enough to bring on an early autumn.

Within less than an hour Alice had returned with four rabbits. Although I offered to help with the skinning and so on, she told me the best thing I could do was hold little Tilda while she got on with it.

'Tilda likes you, she does.' Alice smiled sadly. 'You'd make a really good dad.'

I blushed at the thought, but Alice didn't notice – she was too busy gutting the rabbits. It struck me that she was very resourceful. You'd never go hungry while Alice was around. I was starting to like her more and more.

She soon got a fire going and, after preparing the rabbits, cooked them on spits. Their juices bubbled and hissed in the flames, the tantalizing smell of cooking making my mouth water. I couldn't wait to start eating.

The smell woke Johnson up, and soon he was staring at the rabbits with his mouth open, watching them cook with greedy eyes.

'Give Tilda back to me, Wulf, and I'll feed her while you two eat,' said Alice.

I did as she asked, and she moved a little way from the fire to get some privacy while she fed the child. Johnson and I ate a rabbit each. Mine was delicious, and I could have eaten at least half another one. However, I didn't get the chance: Johnson ate a second rabbit without offering me any, and of course the final rabbit belonged to Alice.

Soon Johnson was snoring again. Who could blame him for grabbing some sleep? He'd been through a terrible ordeal, and we had a difficult night ahead of us, to say the least.

'I don't like to ask this, Wulf, but I'm terribly sleepy. Would you mind holding Tilda again?' Alice asked. 'Wake me in about an hour and then you can sleep too.'

I nodded and took Tilda from her. Alice ate her rabbit and was soon asleep too. She kept her mouth closed and didn't snore. I studied her face. There was no doubt about it: she was really pretty, with her high cheekbones and dark hair. Witch or no witch, no wonder Tom lived with her. I settled down with my back against a tree and supported the baby on my knee. I was very weary, and only meant to close my eyes for a second.

But, without even realizing it, I fell into a deep sleep.

I was awoken by someone tugging the baby from my arms. I realized what had happened, and was ashamed at having dropped asleep holding the child. I expected Alice to be angry – but then I realized that she would never have taken her child from me so roughly.

I turned and stared up into the face of Brother Sabden. He was holding Tilda at arm's length, and glaring down at me. Alice lay on her side, pinned down by two monks, though she was still thrashing wildly. They had already stuffed a gag into her mouth to stop her casting spells, and now they were binding her with ropes.

It was already gloomy in the clearing – late afternoon, I guessed with a sinking heart. I must have slept for hours – no wonder they were able to find us so easily.

'After him!' I heard someone shout, and glanced to my right to see Spook Johnson running away through the trees with three armed men in pursuit.

Then it became a waking nightmare. No brothers from the abbey were to be seen. There were seven killers, including

Brother Sabden, in addition to the three pursuers. Three of those who remained were dressed like monks, while the other three were perhaps mercenaries – just in it for the money. These men were thugs that the Quisitor must have sent for from Blackburn before he died. Either that or Brother Sabden had hired them locally. Under their leader's direction, they worked quickly and efficiently.

Stakes were driven deep into the ground, and we were hauled roughly to our feet and bound to them. Alice's was on my left, but there was an empty stake on my right – probably for Johnson once they'd caught him. They certainly knew what they were doing, but Brother Sabden advised on the finer points as they heaped logs and branches at our feet.

'Put the kindling there!' he instructed. 'No, don't get those big logs too close. We want to see their skin bubble and blister. We need them to die slowly and feel as much pain as possible.'

I was terrified. There was no escape from this. I was going to die. Alice would die too, and I didn't think they'd spare her baby. And it was all my fault for falling asleep when I should have been on watch.

Spook Johnson still hadn't been brought back. I didn't blame him for running. I hoped he'd evaded them.

Alice was fighting against her bonds, but she was tightly bound to the stake. Her eyes were wild and she kept twisting her head from side to side. The gag prevented her from crying out.

They'd taken Tilda somewhere out of sight, but she wasn't making any noise. By now, I thought, she would surely be crying. I just hoped that she was all right and they hadn't harmed her.

In desperation, I too strained at the ropes, trying to free myself. I looked down at the wood piled up below us. They were going to burn us and the pain would be terrible. Suddenly I heard a groaning and a sobbing – and I realized to my shame that I was the one making that pitiful noise.

I took a deep breath and tried to get control of myself, closing my mouth so that I wouldn't cry out. I could now hear Tilda crying in the distance behind us. Alice would be able to hear her too. I saw that her struggles had become even more desperate. I stood there, paralysed by terror, thinking only of myself. I reflected that Alice wasn't thinking of herself at all. She was only concerned about her baby daughter.

Brother Sabden approached us and halted with the toes of his boots touching the wood that would be used to burn us alive. He looked at us arrogantly, as if we were dirt beneath his feet.

'Soon your flesh will burn, and then your souls will plummet into the deepest of the Devil's mansions in Hell. It is there that Satan reserves special torments for witches, and for those priests who die in mortal sin. Once your flesh has been consumed by fire, then your souls will also burn. Remember that as you die in extreme pain, for that pain will be as nothing compared with what you will face then: it will be an agony far more intense – an agony that will never end . . .'

He pointed over our heads and called out to someone behind us. 'Bring the child!' he commanded.

The sound of crying grew louder until another monk came into view and handed the baby to Brother Sabden. He cradled her almost tenderly, a smile on his face.

Taking a step towards Alice, he said, 'It looks so innocent, doesn't it, witch? But appearances can be deceptive. This is the spawn of a witch and an ungodly spook. As such it must die. And yet it is too young to have sinned and so, unlike you, will not suffer eternal pain. In burning this child's flesh, we will purge it of its parentage. Its young soul will be free to fly to God. Thus, if you truly love the child, you should rejoice.'

Brother Sabden approached the cooking fire and held Tilda over the flames. She began to cry even louder as she felt the heat.

I couldn't bear to watch, but neither could I turn my eyes away. I felt sure that Brother Sabden was about to drop Alice's baby into the flames. I was horrified.

However, it soon became clear that he was doing it just to torment Alice. Instead he came back towards us, placed the child on the kindling at Alice's feet and gave her an evil grin. Tilda was crying fit to burst, her face purple.

'Your child will burn at your feet, witch, and your first punishment will be to see it consumed by fire and be unable to help . . .'

Brother Sabden turned to address his men. 'It's time!' he called out. 'Set light to them!'

One of the monks pulled a flaming brand out of the fire and strode towards us, his expression eager and cruel. But then the look on his face suddenly changed. He halted and stared into the trees as if he'd seen or heard something.

Indeed, I too could hear something; something that was lumbering towards us out of the gloom of the trees. Brother Sabden and his men turned towards it.

At first glance it looked like a big shambling bear – but then I saw that it was Spook Johnson. Still wearing Alice's bloodied bandage on his head, he was carrying a huge staff that I could see had been cut very recently: a staff that he had improvised just for this encounter. He held it across his body at an angle of forty-five degrees, in what spooks considered to be the 'defensive position'.

'Well! If it isn't Spook Johnson!' crowed Brother Sabden. 'You are welcome indeed, and just in time to join your friends for the burning!'

With those words, he drew his long sword and his men seized their own weapons. Some also had swords, others had blades or clubs. The one holding the flaming brand threw it down on the grass and snatched up a long spear with a wickedly sharp point. They began to circle Johnson, grinning like it was some sort of game they were about to enjoy.

'Hurt him but don't kill him!' Brother Sabden ordered. 'Cuts and bruises, or even the loss of a few body parts, that's fine, but leave the brute alive for the flames!'

I knew that Spook Johnson had little hope of surviving for more than a few moments against seven armed foes. They circled him on their toes, taunting him. They called him a 'fat porker', and some of them started to grunt and laugh.

Then the joking ended and they decided to get down to business.

They were like lithe wolves about to bring down a cumbersome prey – a lumbering bear that would be ripped into pieces. The staff Johnson was holding had just been cut from a tree. It lacked the silver-alloy blade usually found at the end of a spook's staff. It probably wasn't evenly balanced either, and would be difficult to use effectively. He didn't stand a chance.

Johnson hadn't said a single word. He hadn't reacted in the slightest to the men's shouts and insults. His face was impassive, but I knew that his left eye would be twitching. Then I noticed the fresh blood that soaked the front of his gown. Was it his own blood? If so, he didn't seem to be in any pain. And now that I thought about it – how had he managed to evade his three pursuers?

The wolves closed in now – and then surged towards him as one. Then something truly astonishing happened.

The bear began to dance.

21

THE LEGEND

Crossing the meadow on our way to Salford, I'd seen Tom Ward use his staff against the squire's gamekeeper. I had been impressed by his skill in dealing with him, but realized now that he had been gentle and restrained with his opponent, using minimum force. Now I saw what a spook could do when the odds were against him and his life was on the line.

With the first blow of his staff Spook Johnson slew Brother Sabden. The monk was killed instantly. The sword slipped out of his hand and he was dead before it even hit the ground. Nobody could have survived the force of that blow. It's a wonder his head didn't fall off.

The monk with the spear jabbed it fast and accurately towards Johnson's belly. But it never made contact, because the Spook was no longer there. And he truly was dancing:

he glided around on his toes, performing pirouettes to evade his attackers. It was a wonder to behold – especially in such a big man.

The monk lunged towards Johnson's bulging belly again. This time the Spook retaliated. He rammed the end of his staff into his enemy's mouth. The man's teeth shattered and his mouth spurted with blood. The end of the staff went in so far it must have gone halfway down his throat.

That left five attackers; five would-be killers who were no longer grinning.

Everything was suddenly very quiet. Even Tilda had stopped crying. There was no birdsong. No wind. No rustling of branches. Just the *thwack* of Johnson's staff, making sudden, violent, devastating contact with flesh and bone.

Thwack! Thwack!

And then there *was* another sound.

Caw! Caw! Caw!

It was the raucous cries of crows as they began to alight on the trees above, ravenous black witnesses to each death.

During the time I'd spent working with him, I had judged Johnson to be overweight, greedy, sometimes cruel, and something of a bigot – certainly over-zealous in his pursuit of witches. But he could certainly fight. Until this moment I hadn't realized just how well.

Thwack!

Before my astonished gaze, *The Legend of Spook Johnson* ceased to be a joke. He *was* that legend, suddenly and startlingly come to life.

Thwack!

I realized gratefully that we would not burn here after all.

When the seventh lifeless body fell onto the grass, Johnson laid down his staff and came towards us. Tilda had started to cry again. Very gently, he lifted the baby out of its bed of kindling, held her in the crook of his arm and whispered soothing words to her. As if by magic, she grew calm.

Then, reaching into his gown, he drew out a knife and quickly cut Alice free. She ripped the gag from her mouth and snatched the child into her arms. She checked for harm, and then kissed her on the forehead. Then she kissed Johnson on the cheek.

'Thank you for saving our lives,' she said. 'Especially the life of my child.'

Johnson nodded and then set about cutting me free.

'I'm so sorry for falling asleep, Alice,' I told her as I was released. 'I let you down. Everything that happened was my fault.'

She smiled ruefully, then came across and patted my arm. 'Forget it, Wulf. We were all exhausted – I had no right to ask you to hold Tilda and stay awake. I forgot how young you are. Put it to the back of your mind.'

But it was hard to do so, and I still felt guilty.

I realized that it would soon be dark, but when I suggested burying the bodies of the monks, both Alice and Johnson shook their heads.

'Ain't time for that,' said Alice. 'Need to help Tom, soon as we can.'

'Just leave 'em to the crows, rats and insects,' said Johnson, spitting onto the grass. 'That's all the respect they deserve. Those scum were about to burn you all alive – even that poor defenceless child.'

Although I knew that what he said was true, I wasn't happy to leave these men to rot. I might not wish to be a monk any more, but my time in the abbey had reinforced some of the things my parents had taught me. And burying the dead decently was the proper thing to do, whatever crimes they'd committed.

'Maybe we'll get the chance to come back later,' Alice said, noticing the distress on my face. 'We can bury them then – when it's all over.'

I nodded, and knelt by each body in turn, muttering a quick prayer to St Gertrude, the patron saint of the dead. Then we set off towards the village.

Behind us I could hear the crows already feeding.

As Johnson and I left Alice on the edge of the trees again, she pressed the two feathers into my hands; once more they were bound together and the spell would be activated when I separated them.

The Spook and I walked down the hill together. He was still clutching the huge staff he'd used so effectively against Brother Sabden and his men. He saw me staring at it and gave me a wicked grin. 'This certainly did the job, but it's a shadow of my other weapon. We'll start by getting that back! We'll go straight to that shop and collect what's mine!'

'You think your staff's in there?' I asked.

He nodded. 'My bag too, I hope. Spook Ward said that on entering the shop he was hit with such a sudden, stunning blast of magic that he was knocked clean off his feet. But he was still just about aware of his surroundings, and he saw the witch carrying his bag and staff down some steps.'

It was almost dark and the sky was clear, showing just a few stars to the east. From a distance the shop looked empty and abandoned. But then, as we crossed the street, there was a change. In the space of a footstep, the sky had started to radiate its baleful red glare. We were back in the dangerous underworld of the witch.

Johnson opened the shop door and walked in. As before, the counter and shelves were well stocked with goods, but this time there was no sign of the strange child. A candle flickered on the counter. Johnson snatched it up and walked purposefully through into the back room.

I saw steps leading downwards. Standing at the top of the stairs, I shivered, then followed Spook Johnson. I was developing an aversion to cellars and tunnels. Anywhere down there was probably bad news. Below, we found two rooms: an empty cell, and one that had been used to store items taken from the witch's victims. There were coats and other garments, along with boots, shoes and smelly socks; they had been thrown in a heap on the floor.

The rest of the cell was like a trophy room. Great care had been taken with confiscated weapons, which were stacked neatly against the far wall: swords, clubs, daggers, a couple of longbows and a number of staffs and stout walking sticks. One glance told me which were the two spooks' staffs. Made of rowan wood, they were long and very straight, each with a small button close to the base, which released the silver-alloy blade.

Johnson strode across and seized his staff, then picked up the other one and tossed it towards me. I managed to catch it, though it was heavier than I'd expected.

'You look after Spook Ward's staff for him,' he said. 'It might prove useful against our foes! We'll leave the bags here,' he said, nodding down at two items that sat side by side. 'Once we've killed the witch, we'll come back for them.'

Johnson seemed confident and full of energy again. He began to arm himself with some of the other weapons, sticking two daggers and a club into his belt. Then, to my surprise, he also picked up a longbow.

He saw me looking sceptical. 'Used to be a good shot, though that was years ago. Still, they say the skill never truly leaves you,' he said, slinging a quiver full of arrows over his shoulder and handing me the bow to carry. Typical!

'Right – let's head for that church. We've got a witch to catch . . .'

We climbed the steps, left the shop and continued along the main street. I would have kept a low profile, and concealed myself in any available shadows, but that wasn't Spook Johnson's way. He strode down the centre of the road, as bold as brass, a swagger to his walk, as if challenging the witch to do her worst. I wondered how long it would be before she did just that.

He beckoned me forward to walk alongside him. As I did so, to my astonishment he beamed at me and clapped me hard on the shoulder.

'You did well, boy, killing that ugly little guzzler. You saved my life and I owe you. I doubt you'll be going back to that abbey after this,' he said. 'You'll need a job, and I might have the very thing for you. I'm looking for a new apprentice, and the job's yours if you want it.'

This was a surprise! I had thought he considered me useless.

'I don't think I'd be very good at it,' I told him.

'Nonsense. You were the only monk in that abbey that met all the criteria I set. You weren't the best writer they had, but there was something about you that was more important than that. You've seen how following me around is dangerous, and you need certain abilities to help keep you relatively safe when facing the dark. Luckily for you, you've got the main qualification that a spook's apprentice needs. When I was looking for a scribe who fulfilled all my requirements, the Abbot assured me that it was recorded in the abbey archives. You're the seventh son of a seventh son!'

When we reached the church, my head was still whirling with what Johnson had told me. I hadn't been aware that I was the seventh son of a seventh son, but the more I thought about it, the more I realized it might be possible. My father had come from a very large family, but a lot of his brothers had died before he was born, and I didn't know how many there had been. I had three older brothers, but I knew that, very early in her marriage, my mother had lost children in childbirth or soon afterwards. Those memories were painful and she never talked about them – and I supposed they could have all been boys.

If this was indeed true, then as far as I knew, being the seventh son of a seventh son made you fit for only one job: that of a spook. I didn't want to be a monk any more, and it was probably better than being a farmer. But it was also a very dangerous occupation.

My thoughts returned to the present as we entered the church. Soon we were below the vault and making our way along the tunnels.

'At each fork I chose the right one until I found you and Spook Ward,' I told Johnson. 'I did that so that if I had to retrace my steps I'd be less likely to get lost.'

I didn't mention the part the saint had played in this decision. In any case, Johnson would most likely tell me to shut up, and ignore my advice, but he quickly proved me wrong.

'Given that I was brought unconscious down these tunnels, and have no memory of the route, we'll do as you suggest, boy. It sounds like common sense to me,' he said.

So we did just that. From the first doorway emerged the distinctive sounds of sipping and slurping. Johnson went into the room, his staff held high. Instantly there was a terrible shrill scream, and when I followed him in I saw that he'd already pinned one of the ugly little brain guzzlers to the side of the trough where it had been feeding. Then he stabbed it again with the silver-alloy blade until it was squirming and twitching in a dark pool of its own blood. Within seconds it lay still.

'What a pity that there's only one of the little blighters here,' Spook Johnson complained, shaking his head. 'But I'm sure I'll soon get the chance to kill a few more!'

Finally we reached the room where Spook Johnson and Tom Ward had been held captive. This time it was empty of both prisoners and brain guzzlers, so we hurried on along the tunnels, always turning right.

There were a lot of forks, and I was growing dispirited. Too much time had passed, I thought to myself. How could Tom Ward possibly have survived so long? The situation began to look more and more hopeless. If we did find him down here, he might already be possessed, a guzzler inside his skull controlling his every motion. He might now be one of those in thrall to the witch, a threat to us rather than a friend.

It seemed there were no more rooms – just endless tunnels. However, I noticed that things were changing: previously the tunnels had been oddly empty of life; now life in its many forms began to share the tunnels with us. Long-tailed grey rats scurried away from us into the shadows, green lizards clung to the ceiling and walls, and bats flitted close to our heads; not to mention the insects that crawled and flew, buzzing and settling on any exposed flesh. And the temperature seemed to be getting warmer.

This was both alarming and uncomfortable, and our journey seemed without end. I began to fear that we were in some sort of magical maze, bewitched by a spell that was sending us in circles. Then, finally, we reached the end of the tunnels. I was relieved, but immediately apprehensive about what new monstrosities we might find.

Suddenly, ahead of us, the tunnel came to an end. We stopped and peered at the stone steps that led upwards. Johnson started to climb them and I followed at his heels, still clutching the bow and Tom Ward's staff. Burdened as I was, I began to fall further and further behind. It was hard work climbing those steps, and I soon became breathless. Why were there so many of them? I wondered. Surely we couldn't have travelled so far underground?

I'd been expecting Johnson to call down to me, bad-tempered because of my slow progress. But when he finally uttered something, it was a cry of wonder at what he was seeing, rather than a reprimand.

As I approached the end of the staircase, I saw that the sky was still radiating the same red light. When I emerged to stand at Spook Johnson's side, I also gasped at what I saw.

We saw trees – three concentric circles of them – but not ones I recognized from the County. They surrounded a large building that rose above them, gleaming white despite the red light. It seemed to be made of marble. With all its pillars, it was as imposing as a cathedral, though the architecture was very different. I thought I had once seen an illustration of a similar building in a book in the abbey. It was a temple, typical of those found in the country called Greece.

Moreover, I realized that the air was much warmer than it had been before we entered the church; hotter even than the very best of County summers.

'Have I been here before?' Johnson asked. He was clearly just as stunned as I was, and simply thinking aloud as he stared at the white marble building.

He gave a grunt, shook his head like a bear plagued with flies, and started walking. Talking of flies, beneath the trees swarmed great clouds of them, rising and falling in perpetual motion. I followed close at Johnson's heels, and within moments we were passing beneath the branches of the second circle of trees. As we did so, a dark shadow swept across the sky from left to right. We both glanced upwards and I caught a glimpse of something flying overhead.

What was it? It was surely too large to be a bird. It was certainly no County bird; indeed it didn't appear to have any wings. But we weren't on earth, were we? I reflected. Who knew what devilish creatures might dwell here.

We came out into the open, and again saw that dark shape, which was now flying directly towards us. I heard Johnson gasp. We were looking at something impossible.

By now I knew a bit about witches. I knew that they were dangerous and that there were many types – not only had I read about them in Johnson's library, I'd now come face to face with quite a few. They were all female, usually devious and dangerous, and mostly malignant. They fought each other, and preyed on the ordinary folk of the County. Some drank human blood; others coveted bones or kept familiars.

They were incredibly strong and fast, and many could cast powerful spells.

Yet there was one thing that none of them did; one thing they all had in common. They couldn't fly.

But this witch could. I could now see her concave face against the red sky, her predatory eyes staring down at us as she passed overhead.

The witch was flying on a broomstick.

22

ONE OF THE IMMORTALS

'Give me the bow!' Spook Johnson snapped, casting his staff aside.

With trembling hands, I passed him the huge longbow. He stared at it, then looked up at the sky again. The witch was flying in a wide curve that would soon bring her back towards us. She would probably pass directly overhead. This time she might blast us with a spell.

Johnson reached back over his shoulder and pulled an arrow from the quiver. Then he nocked it, drew back the cord and started to track the witch, carefully adjusting his aim, his eyes focused on her. I wondered if his claim to have been a good shot was just another of his boasts.

I soon saw that it wasn't.

Spook Johnson released the arrow. It flew towards the witch with a *whoosh*, and buried itself in her side. She gave a scream and fell off the broomstick, arms and legs flapping like broken wings.

It was a long way down, and she hit the ground with a terrible thud. I was certain nobody could have survived that fall, but Johnson thrust the bow at me, picked up his staff and ran towards the body. I heard the click as the silver-alloy blade emerged from the tip of the staff. If the witch wasn't already dead, he intended to finish her off. He was taking no chances. And he was right not to.

Just as Johnson reached her, the witch came onto her knees, clutching her side, trying to tug the arrow free. Her face was twisted in agony; her blood splattered the ground.

Spook Johnson showed her no mercy, and I didn't blame him. For, although she was hurt and temporarily weak, how long would it take her to recover? I remembered the human flesh and blood in the trough from which her familiars were greedily feeding, and wondered who those poor victims were. I remembered the way she'd blasted us with dark magic when I escaped from her lair with Johnson. No. She was a dangerous predator and could not be allowed to live.

Johnson stabbed her with the blade in his staff at least half a dozen times. She twitched a little, and then lay still.

The witch's death had been horrible to watch, but it had brought the danger to an end. I was filled with a great sense of relief. It was over, the witch was defeated, and we could search for Tom Ward relatively unhindered. No doubt Johnson thought the same, but we were both wrong.

Just as Johnson started to walk back towards me, a confident grin on his face, we heard a terrible noise.

We turned to look at the witch's body, and stared as the top of her skull fell backwards onto the ground. Inside was something that was not a brain. It was one of the ugly little familiars – it must have guzzled the brain of the witch and possessed her!

The creature crawled out and began to dart away. It was fast, but Spook Johnson was faster. Once again he was dancing. Suddenly the guzzler halted, turned and called out in that strange, throaty, deep voice.

'Mercy! Mercy!' it cried.

Spook Johnson didn't know the meaning of the word. He impaled the guzzler on the end of his blade, shook it free, then stabbed it twice more until it lay still in a pool of its own blood.

Then he turned to me and scratched his head in puzzlement. 'I'm really not sure what we're dealing with here,' he admitted. 'There must be more than just a witch to contend with. Is there one evil mind behind all this, or are these familiars working for themselves? That would be totally new. And I don't like the look of that either,' he said, gesturing towards the white marble building. 'It looks Greek to me, and I saw something similar when I was just a lad. Remember how I told you about that witch who turned me into a pig? Well, she lived in a pagan temple just like that. I'm sure it can't be the same witch – Old Gregory killed her – but maybe this witch could be similar.'

Johnson had previously told me that *he* had killed the witch, not Gregory. He'd obviously been exaggerating his own prowess, as usual – but now wasn't the time to mention it. Then I remembered the strange little girl whom I'd met twice in the shop.

'The giant and the witch were both possessed by familiars,' I said, thinking aloud. 'But what about that little girl I talked to? I was told that I was too small to be a host to one of those brain guzzlers. Surely she's too small too? Whoever she is, she's not possessed. So what's she doing?'

'Well, the answer might be somewhere in there!' Johnson said, pointing through the trees towards the temple again.

I sighed. He was probably right.

I had a bad feeling as I approached the seven marble pillars that formed the colonnade. Beyond them, everything was very dark. This was a pagan temple – no place for a noviciate monk. Maybe some dark god or demon dwelt within it?

Johnson came to a halt, facing the two central pillars. I could hear the buzzing of insects and the slithering and pattering of small things inside the temple. I also sensed something waiting further inside. Something dangerous and predatory.

Before I could put my fears into words, Spook Johnson stepped forward into the darkness. I had no choice but to follow.

Soon the darkness was total, but I could hear Johnson's boots ringing on the flags ahead of me, so I followed the sound. I could also hear the occasional buzzing close to my head, but there were fewer flies than before. No doubt that was because of all the spiders. I didn't see any – it was too dark – but I could certainly feel their webs. They hung down like curtains, and I couldn't avoid touching them. I was carrying the staff and bow, so it was difficult to brush them off me. Ahead of me I could hear Johnson cursing and muttering.

Suddenly there was a glimmer of light ahead, and at last I saw that we had reached the very back of the temple. There was a single torch hanging from a bracket on the far wall. Below it was a dais of white marble, upon which stood a large black marble throne with a red cushion. A small figure sat perched upon it.

Thanks to the torch, we could now see the grey webs hanging down, several feet above our heads, and within them large black spiders scuttled hither and thither, pouncing on each trapped fly.

As we approached, I saw that the figure on the throne was the little girl with red hair whom I'd talked to in the village shop. Her hair was exactly the same shade of red as the cushion, and she was wearing a long purple dress that was far too large for her. The material flowed over the jutting points of her shoes to cascade down onto the dais below her.

She stared at me with big round eyes and gave a sly smile.

'Back again, priest? What do you want this time?' she demanded.

'I want Tom Ward,' I answered. 'And I want you to show me where he is.'

'And what do *you* want, Spook?' asked the child with a frown, turning to Johnson. Her tone was impudent and I sensed him bristling with anger. I wanted to warn him – this was clearly no ordinary child.

'Mind your manners, girl,' he chided her, taking a step nearer the throne. 'I don't know who you are, why you're here or what you think you're playing at, but if you show us where Spook Ward is, we'll be on our way.'

'Take care how you speak to *me*,' said the child, her voice deepening with anger. 'This is *my* domain and *anything* is possible here. What I choose shall come to pass. We have met before, you foolish man. You were just a boy then, but I have a long memory, and neither forgive nor forget.'

Johnson opened his mouth to make an angry retort; then, instead of words, he uttered a shrill squeal and a snort. He had often snorted at me before, but this was different. It was a truly animal sound that couldn't possibly emerge from a human throat. I looked at him in astonishment, and saw that his face was moving and changing, the nose starting to thicken.

There were crackling, sucking, stretching noises accompanying that change, as if bone, flesh and gristle were being repositioned. His nose had now elongated and fattened into a long piggy snout, wet at the tip, and his cheeks had bloated, making his eyes seem smaller. His face now resembled that of a pig more than a human being's.

Horrified, I stared at the child in fear. I'd witnessed a possessed witch flying on a broomstick, and now Johnson with his altered face ... these were displays of immense power. I'd increasingly thought that Alice was our last chance – that, if things went badly, she might somehow save us. Now I realized it was hopeless: Alice could never challenge such hellish magic.

But then hope flared within me again. Perhaps these powers only worked here in this underworld domain. If this witch entered our world, perhaps she wouldn't be so powerful. It was worth a try. I had to get us out of the temple. That was our only hope of survival.

Spook Johnson had dropped his staff and was now on his hands and knees, snuffling at the ground, mucus dripping from his wet snout.

I was terrified that she would change me into a pig next, so I quickly started talking.

'Spook Johnson told me that, when he was younger, he was changed into a pig,' I said, aware of the tremor in my voice. 'Are you the same powerful witch who did that to him?'

I suddenly saw that the child's legs were longer now, the pointy shoes sliding down beneath the purple dress and extending towards the dais. Her body was filling out, and her face was changing too; it was starting to mature. Within moments it was a woman who was sat facing me. She still had red hair and green eyes, but everything else had changed.

'I'm no mere witch, priest!' she rebuked me. 'I am a goddess, the most powerful of the beings who dwell within the dark. It's true that, when I first met Johnson, I possessed the body of a witch. When she died, slain by John Gregory, I was driven from her body. That spook was ever a thorn in the side of the dark. Finally he too is dead, although his former apprentices, Ward and Johnson, have continued to bother us . . . until now.'

Her lip curled and she spat on the floor close to Spook Johnson's head. He came forward, and his pink tongue began to lick at the globule of spit.

'Pitiful, isn't he?' she said, coming to her feet; and all at once a long, grey-shafted spear appeared in her hands. I hadn't even seen her pick it up. It was as if she'd plucked it out of clean air. The point gleamed in the torchlight, looking wickedly sharp. Suddenly she drove it hard into Johnson's right shoulder and twisted it savagely.

He let out a shrill squeal of pain, exactly like a pig in a slaughterhouse, and, still on all fours, ran around in circles. I could see the blood starting to soak through his gown.

'*That* is his punishment for destroying my creature!' the goddess cried.

I tore my eyes away from poor Johnson and stared at her, saying nothing. Did she mean the witch that Johnson had killed? First the Abbot and the Quisitor had sought to destroy the County spooks. Now this evil goddess wished to do the same. What was it about them that made the servants of both Heaven and Hell seek their destruction? I wondered.

'Would you still like to meet the other spook called Ward?' she demanded.

'Yes,' I replied, seeing a glimmer of hope. I still had the feathers that Alice had given me. If Tom was near enough, I might have a chance to touch both him and Johnson, and use the spell to get us out of this terrifying underworld.

A hooded figure shuffled forward into the light cast by the torch. I realized that he had been standing there in the shadows all along, probably listening to what was being said. He approached until he was near enough to touch, and then threw back his hood.

It was Tom Ward.

One of the Immortals

He was looking at me, but there was a strange expression on his face. His eyes were glassy and he seemed bewildered. Then he knelt at the feet of the goddess, who grinned at me and placed her hand on the top of his head.

Suddenly she gripped his hair, bunching it tightly in her left fist. She jerked her hand upwards, and the top third of Tom Ward's skull was lifted away. The brain was gone, replaced by one of the ugly little familiars.

We had arrived too late to save him.

THE MAGI

I could only gaze in horror and sadness at what had been done to Tom. I allowed the bow and staff to fall from my hands, then reached into my pocket and closed my fingers over the feathers. Johnson and I could be free of this place in a moment, but the thought of having to face Alice with such terrible news was almost unbearable.

'This is someone who will cause me no further trouble.' The goddess smirked.

I groaned in anguish. 'Poor Tom. He didn't deserve this!' I murmured to her.

'Are you sure about that?' she asked, her lip curling in contempt as she replaced the top of his skull, hiding the ugly familiar from view. 'What other fate should be reserved for an enemy of the dark who challenges a goddess? But don't worry, little monk. Things in my domain are not always what they seem. Look again at this wretch!'

I stared at Tom's face, which had begun to twitch, eyes blinking rapidly, mouth convulsing. As I watched, it changed until it was no longer his. It had aged; the hair was grey, the face gaunt, the cheeks sunken, and a small white moustache adorned the upper lip.

'This is Mr Batley, the shopkeeper,' the goddess told me. 'He had a bit of a headache for a while, but now he is much happier and will age no more. Of course,' she said, giving a wicked smile, 'he is no longer quite himself!'

How true that was. Mr Batley had now ceased to exist, his mind devoured and now possessed by a brain guzzler. I felt sorry for the poor man, but was simultaneously relieved to find out that it wasn't Tom. It seemed that this woman liked playing games; she had enjoyed causing me anguish.

She came to her feet. 'Follow me, priest,' she commanded, walking away into the darkness.

I hesitated and looked down at Johnson, who was still snuffling at the floor, licking up his own blood as it dripped from his shoulder. I didn't want to leave him in such a helpless condition.

'If you want to see Ward again, follow me *now*!' the goddess called back imperiously. 'Soon it will be too late.'

This time I followed her into the darkness. Apart from the wound, Johnson didn't seem to be in any immediate danger but, if she were to be believed, Tom was. However, I needed the two spooks close together so that I could use the magical feathers. I would have to hope that Tom and I could somehow come back and fetch Johnson.

It was so dark that I couldn't see my hand in front of my face, but I could hear the woman's shoes clip-clopping across the flags ahead of me. As I walked, I was gradually aware of an unpleasant smell, which grew stronger with each step. It was like walking into a farmyard, only worse. All at once there was light ahead, three flickering candles, and they lit a scene that halted me in my tracks.

I saw a long table spread with a pristine white cloth; the three fat black candles set in golden candlesticks showed me that the table was heaped with food – fruits and dishes of cold meats, and a simmering pot of what looked like a meat stew.

There were three chairs: one at the head of the table, and two more facing each other. Tom was seated on one of them. His hands were flat on the tablecloth, palms down, but there was something wrong with his face. I took a step closer, then recoiled in horror.

He had no eyes, no mouth. There was not even the hint of lips, just a smooth expanse of skin from nose to chin.

'Tom! Tom!' I called. He did not respond in any way. He was immobile, but for the slight rise and fall of his chest, which showed me that he was at least breathing.

'He's in a deep, dreamless sleep and will be unable to dine with us,' the goddess told me as she sat down at the head of the table. There was no sign of the spear. Had she cast it away into the darkness? I wondered.

She stared up at me, her eyes full of cruelty. 'He has not *yet* come to permanent harm, so do not concern yourself. Take a seat. Try the meat. It's delicious . . .'

Numb and still staring at Tom, I sat down. The woman began to ladle the contents of the pot onto the plate in front of her, then reached across and heaped my plate with more of the steaming stew.

I leaned forward and sniffed the food, wondering what kind of meat it was. I could smell nothing because of the strong farmyard odour. I remembered the familiars eating from the long tray and slurping up the blood of their victims. Was this the same human flesh and blood? I sat there, trembling in horror.

'Eat it up quickly! Don't let it go cold,' the woman chided me.

I didn't dare refuse her directly in case it made her angry, but I didn't want to risk eating the meat either, so I tried to divert her by asking a question: 'Why did you take the shape of a young girl?'

'Why not?' she retorted. 'What could be better than to look out through the eyes of a child, full of wonder at what she sees? And what better way to disguise one's true capabilities? It is always better to let others underestimate you.'

The goddess's arms were bare and her purple dress now hung low about her shoulders, revealing a wide expanse of flesh. A strange movement drew my attention. I tried not to stare, and just observed it out of the corner of my eye. It seemed that worms or snakes were moving beneath her alabaster skin: she was crawling with inner lives, host to slimy reptiles that slithered through her veins and arteries, parasites that swam within her immortal blood.

She glanced at my plate again but, before she could speak, I asked another question. 'Why did you kill Mr Batley?'

She placed her palms together, making a steeple. 'He was such a foolish man, so full of self-importance. He was vain too, always combing his hair and smoothing his silly moustache. And mortals do not last long. When he became an old man and was no longer attractive to me, I put a stop to that. I loved Mr Batley once, but I have always been unlucky with men. They have always been a great disappointment to me . . .'

I didn't know what to say. She was frowning and staring at my plate again.

'Men are extremely stupid,' she said, glaring at me. 'Don't you agree?'

I didn't. I thought there were *some* stupid men in the world, and *some* stupid women as well, but I thought it best not to contradict her.

Now I caught sight of movement in her hair. I thought I could see tiny red mites moving among the red strands; minuscule specks of life. Was it those tiny living entities that gave her hair its vivid red colour?

'I lived in the village long ago when it was thriving,' the woman continued, 'and I was happy for a while. I kept my needs in check. But soon I became weary. Boredom is the prime enemy of an immortal. When Mr Batley realized that I was using my familiars to possess his friends and neighbours, he became very unhappy. I could endure his accusations no longer, so I gave him a headache, and now he has no more cause to chide me. Thus it all ends happily ever after—'

Before she could go on, I asked another question – something else that I was curious about.

'That witch with the moon face was very strange. She reminded me of an illustration I once saw in a children's book that I was told to copy . . .'

'Of course, she did, priest. I made her that way because it pleased me to do so. I formed her flesh from clay and blood, then breathed life into her before placing her in a story which I brought to life. All life is a narrative if you have the wit to see it, though it can ramble in uncontrolled directions. However, a goddess can shape a story for her own delight. The witch was a creature crafted to my design, but in time she became wilful, wishing to make decisions for herself. So she too suffered a headache and became compliant to my will. I always get what I want in the end. Now I have answered enough questions. Eat your meat, priest. I shall not tell you again.'

I pushed the plate away. 'I can't!' I cried, my revulsion turning to anger. 'What kind of meat is it?' I demanded.

She shrugged. 'What does it matter once the creature is dead? Why let it go to waste? Human flesh is very similar in taste to pork,' she said, putting a large piece of meat in her mouth and starting to chew.

There was bile in my throat and I almost retched. She saw my discomfort and smiled. 'Well, if you're not going to eat, you might as well leave,' she said. 'After all, all you need do is take hold of those feathers in your pocket and pull them apart.'

She had known about the feathers all along! How? Could she read my mind? But then I remembered that the witch with the moon face had seen us when we escaped last time. The goddess would have realized then that we had used some type of magic. No doubt the spell was known to her.

Her smile widened. 'It might hasten things if you go back now . . .'

'I'll leave only if I can take both spooks with me,' I retorted.

The woman's grin grew even more sly. 'Eventually the spooks may leave as well, but only when Alice Deane gives me what I want . . .'

I was shocked. What on earth did she want with Alice? I wondered.

She paused as if waiting for me to ask the obvious question, but I said nothing. I was too stunned. Alice was known to her. It seemed that the goddess was aware of much that had been happening out there in the world.

The woman grew tired of waiting. 'If she gives me her child, all of you can go free,' she said.

'Her child?' I asked in astonishment.

'Yes, her child. Didn't you hear me the first time?'

'Why do you want her child?'

'You ask too many questions, little priest. I am sure that Alice Deane will know why I've gone to such lengths to ensure that her child falls into my hands. I require the blood that flows through her tiny veins – such exquisite blood. It is the lineage that is so important. Such a special mother and such a truly astonishing bloodline from the father. It is unique, and it holds the key to so much power. Now – go now and pass on my message to Alice Deane!'

I hesitated. Could I reach across and touch Tom Ward, and at least take him back with me? But, as I delayed, the face of the goddess grew even more furious; things twitched beneath her skin, making her lips pout and pulling at the skin below her eyes.

'Do my bidding now or die here, torn to pieces by my little pets,' she told me.

There was a deep growl from the darkness beyond her, and then a pair of glowing eyes moved towards me. Now I finally knew the source of the farmyard stink. I saw the head of a giant cat, its shoulders the height of the goddess's, its coat patterned with symmetrical black-and-white stripes. It opened its mouth and roared, its foul breath washing over me. Then came two answering growls from behind me.

'I call my pets the Magi because each of the three was once a human king, wielding his malignant power over the poor humans he ruled. Now I have given them a shape that better suits their nature and their purpose in serving me. If I were to set them on you, it would be quite entertaining. You see, they are anything but predictable. They might play with you like a cat with a mouse, delighting in your pain until they become bored and finish you off by disembowelling you with their hind legs. Or they might tear out your throat, giving you moments of agony as your blood gushes forth and you struggle for breath. Or they might be merciful. It is rare, but it happens. Mercy is a quick death. They might seize your head in powerful jaws and crush your skull like an egg. It is messy but most effective . . .'

I was terrified, my hand trembling so much that I couldn't get it into my pocket. The goddess smiled at my discomfort.

'One more thing, priest. Be sure to tell Alice Deane who I am. My name is Circe. I am one of the Old Gods. She will hear my name, and know better than to thwart my will.'

I still couldn't get my shaking hand into my pocket to reach the feathers. The woman saw what I was trying to do, and threw back her head and laughed. Then she hissed in fury and pointed her forefinger at me. There was a flash of light, and a pain like fire in my blood as she blasted me with her magic.

I felt a surge of fear as my mind was plunged into darkness.

My last terrified thought was that she had slain me.

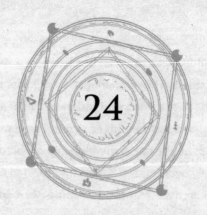

24

A YEAR AND A DAY

Instead of killing me, she'd lost patience, used her own magic and sent me back to deliver her message.

It was late afternoon, the sun already sinking into the western sky. I was lying just outside the shop of the deserted village. Time must have passed at a different rate in Circe's underworld. There, it had still been night. Out here it was much colder than it had been in the temple, and I could smell wood smoke. I sensed the approach of autumn and the long freezing winter that waited beyond it.

I clambered unsteadily to my feet and began walking up the hill to where Alice was waiting. I had escaped the lair of the goddess but left both spooks behind, still subject to her merciless will. And now I had to break that news to Alice.

She'd made a small fire and I sat cross-legged before it, shivering and staring into the flames as I related most of what had occurred. I told her how Circe had transformed Johnson, but I didn't mention that she had tricked me into thinking that Tom was no more, his body merely a vehicle for a brain guzzler. I thought that would have been too upsetting. Nor did I describe how Tom's eyes and mouth had been erased; I just said he'd been asleep. After all, Circe had claimed that he hadn't been harmed permanently. I just had to hope it was true. Finally I gave Alice Circe's message.

While I was talking, she had been pacing backwards and forwards, Tilda cradled tightly against her chest. She listened but did not speak. She listened and wept.

'What will you do?' I asked, after completing my account.

Alice let out a deep sob, then came to a halt facing me.

'Circe is a powerful goddess; she's cruel and dangerous – no doubt about it. Her magic is much stronger than mine. She plays with humans, and often turns them into beasts – like the Magi. But I could never surrender Tilda to her. Even though I love Tom more than my life, I couldn't do that. A mother's first duty is to protect her child – ain't that so? But . . . there may yet be a way to save them both. It'll mean a terrible sacrifice, but once it's done I might have a chance of saving Tom and Johnson. We can do nothing until nightfall though.'

Alice paced and muttered to herself until the fire had died down and was just glowing embers. The light began to fail, and she finally sat down beside me, still cradling Tilda, and together we stared into the gloom, listening to the wind sighing through the trees.

'I'm glad you didn't eat the food Circe offered,' Alice said at last.

'I think it was human flesh and blood,' I answered. 'If so, Circe is a cannibal.'

She nodded. 'Yes, she is that. To her, the flesh of humans tastes even better than pork. She likes to feed her guests, but it's said that those who dine with her are doomed to repeat it one day. But then it's their own flesh that simmers in the pot. Could be there's some truth in it. Anyway, ain't good to eat what Circe offers. Glad you refused, Wulf.'

Alice fell silent and I thought about the lucky escape I'd had.

'Are you waiting for something?' I asked, my voice just a whisper.

'I'm waiting for some*one*. You must hold your tongue, Wulf. You don't need to be afraid. No harm will come to you.'

She pulled something out of her skirt pocket and breathed upon it three times, then muttered something, her voice too low for me to hear the words. I couldn't see properly what it was, but for a second the embers of the fire were reflected on it, and I knew that it was a mirror.

The darkness intensified; the glow from the embers began to fade. From somewhere in the distance came the screech of an owl, but after that all fell silent; even the breeze died. It seemed as if the whole world was holding its breath.

Then a tall figure came striding out of the darkness towards the fire – though this did nothing to disturb the silence. The dying embers cast forth little light, but the person approaching appeared to be glowing, radiating some kind of light, and I could see every terrible detail. It was a woman, but she was more demon than mortal, and had the bearing of a warrior. Her hair was dark and her skirt was split, each half bound to a thigh. She wore a necklace of white bones, and there were straps across her body holding sheathed blades.

'Can you help me, Grimalkin?' Alice called to her across the embers of the fire. 'My need is desperate.'

My heart lurched at the name – *Grimalkin*. Tom had told me she'd been the witch assassin of the Malkin clan and that he'd once formed an alliance with her – a way of dealing with their common enemies. However, he'd also told me that she was dead. Could this be the same witch? I wondered, terrified. Could the dead come back and walk the earth in the flesh? The Church said no, but I knew all too well how wrong the Church had been before.

Grimalkin's gaze moved from Alice to me, then back to Alice, and a shiver of fear ran down my spine.

When she replied, her mouth was terrible to behold, her teeth filed to points and the timbre of her voice barely human.

'*I will do what I can, child. Follow me . . .*'

She turned and began to walk away from the trees into the darkness. Alice followed, still clutching Tilda.

They were away for no longer than a few moments. When they returned, they came to a halt a few paces short of the fire.

'*Farewell,*' said Grimalkin. '*One year and one day from this night I will seek you out. If you still live, we will conclude our business.*'

'And if I am already dead?' Alice asked.

'*Then I will make the best provision that I can.*'

'It is enough. I am content,' said Alice. 'I thank you for your help.'

Grimalkin walked back into the darkness and Alice approached me. She looked awful – but it seemed she'd made up her mind.

'Be brave, Wulf. I'm sorry, but you got to enter that underworld a fourth time. Still, you don't need to worry – I'll be at your side,' she said with a wry smile.

'We're going now?' I asked, getting to my feet.

'Yes,' Alice said, and she turned and headed towards the wood. 'We have to free Tom and Johnson, don't we?'

Did she intend to give Tilda to Circe, despite all she'd said about a mother protecting her child? It was a question I was too afraid to ask, so instead I asked her about Grimalkin: was she truly a witch assassin?

Alice nodded without looking at me. She seemed distracted, deep in thought.

'But Tom said that she was dead . . .'

As we entered the trees, Alice halted and turned to face me. 'Yes, Wulf, she's dead. She died fighting a god and her spirit fell into the dark—'

'Into Hell?' I interrupted.

'Call it what you like, it's the place where witches go after death – they and other souls who've succumbed to the dark. The Old Gods such as Circe – they're there too – and all sorts of demons. A few of these demons and Old Gods can leave the dark briefly, but most of 'em are bound there. That Circe is very powerful, but she's still bound to the dark. That's why she created an underworld – so she can prey upon humans – that's what she likes to do, ain't it?'

'And Grimalkin is able to do the same? Can she leave the dark?' I asked.

'Yes, for a short while. But she ain't got no underworld, and can only come during the hours of darkness. The light of the sun would destroy her, see. She was formidable in life and she's just as dangerous now that she's dead. I had an alliance with Grimalkin too, I did, and I asked for her help tonight.'

'Could she defeat Circe?' I wondered.

Alice shook her head. 'That's not likely – it ain't something I'd want to put to the test. She could defend herself, that's for sure, but Circe is extremely old and powerful. As for my own strength – I wouldn't like to chance that. Even the most powerful witch can't do much against a goddess like her. Now come on – lead me to Circe and I'll do what must be done.'

The tears had gone and Alice's face was filled with determination as she held her baby to her. Once more I walked towards the underworld.

25

GREEN-TALONED HANDS

With a heavy heart I guided Alice towards the temple of Circe.

I feared the outcome of their meeting. Did she really intend to swap her child, sacrificing Tilda for the freedom of Tom Ward and Spook Johnson? I wondered. Or did she intend to fight the goddess and meet magic with magic, even though she doubted her chances of victory?

When we reached the village street, the sky changed, the stars replaced by the menacing red glow that heralded our arrival in Circe's underworld. I guided Alice to the church, then led her down the steps into the endless tunnels, always choosing the right-hand path, and we made good progress.

We were cautious and checked each of the rooms as we passed, but saw none of the familiars or any other agent of the goddess. At last we climbed the final steps that brought us up just outside the first of the three circles of trees surrounding the temple. Once again I was aware of an alien warmth and the buzzing of insects. As we walked through the trees, I began to sweat – with exertion, heat and fear.

We passed the dead witch with her open skull, and the little familiar lying stabbed and bloody in the grass.

'The work of Spook Johnson?' asked Alice, raising her eyebrows.

'She was flying on her broomstick and he shot her out of the sky with a bow and arrow,' I replied.

'We should never underestimate that man,' she said, and shook her head. 'Ain't right to underestimate Circe either, especially here. She gave a possessed witch the power to fly. Here she makes what's not possible become possible. This is her lair and she's dangerous here – no doubt about it. What we're about to do is full of risk.'

I still didn't understand what it was that we were going to do, but I knew better than to ask questions now. Alice needed to focus on her plan, not be distracted by me.

We passed through the trees and came at last to the colonnade. Here we halted, peering between the pillars and into the threatening darkness.

'I'm not sure I can find the place where Tom was sitting at the table,' I warned Alice. 'It seemed to be a long way. It must be somewhere at the very back of the temple.'

'Wherever we walk we'll find what we seek,' said Alice. 'Ain't nothing more certain than that. Circe will come to us. So from now on keep behind me at all times, Wulf. It's my turn to lead the way, and whatever I tell you, do it at once and without question. We'll have just seconds to get this done and escape. Don't try to interfere or change the outcome in any way. Your life will depend on it, that's for sure. All our lives will. Do you understand?'

'Yes.'

'Then follow me.'

We stepped into the darkness. Alice was taking slow, deliberate steps, holding Tilda protectively, and I followed close at her heels. Then something white loomed at us out of the darkness, causing me a moment of apprehension, but as I passed by I saw that it was only a marble sculpture set upon a pillar. It was a carved head of a woman, but instead of hair, snakes writhed from her scalp. Then I saw another pillar with a larger bust: the figure had a muscular chest and arms, but instead of a human head it had that of a horned bull. Were these representations of demons? I wondered.

Then, far ahead, I saw flickering candles, and once again I smelled that farmyard reek. Those big cat-like beasts must be somewhere close by.

This time there was no table laid before us, just that large black throne. Still in the form of an adult, Circe was seated on it, a gloating smile on her face. Sitting on the flagged floor, about five paces in front of the throne, were both spooks. They even had their staffs and bags beside them.

Tom's mouth and eyes looked normal again, but there was a bewildered expression on his face – and on Johnson's too. It was as if they didn't quite know where they were or what was happening. Johnson's gown was caked with dried blood from the wound to his shoulder. However, it seemed to have stopped bleeding and his face was human again.

Then I glimpsed something that made my legs tremble with fear. The three giant cat-beasts were lying sprawled behind the throne. Their savage power was evident in their sleek striped coats and the muscles bunched in their shoulders. One opened its mouth wide and gave a yawn, allowing me to glimpse the razor-sharp yellow teeth, the fangs long enough to curl down over its lower jaw.

'After I've gone past him, stand very close to Tom and stay there, Wulf!' Alice whispered to me in a low voice as she approached the throne with Tilda.

'You are so wise to accede to my wishes,' Circe said, beckoning Alice towards her. 'As you can see, I have kept to my side of the exchange. Both these wretches are free to return with you.'

It was then that Alice came to a halt and gazed directly at Circe. Then she spoke, her voice loud and clear, and filled with defiance.

'Who are you to covet my child?' she demanded. 'This is the blood of my blood, the flesh of my flesh, and she belongs to me. Goddess you may be, but I am her mother!'

Circe did not seem annoyed by Alice's outburst. She gave a gloating smile and replied mildly. 'Of course you are her mother, but the child is only half you. The blood of that wretch there also flows through her veins,' she said, casting a glance towards Tom Ward, who still looked confused. If he was able to hear the voices of Circe and Alice, it was clear that he did not understand what was being said.

'Lamia blood and that of a seventh son of a seventh son are added to the concoction,' said Circe, her voice rising. 'It is a liquid fit for a goddess, a true red nectar of power. That is why I desire it. Give to me what is my due!'

The reference to lamia blood puzzled me. How could Tom possibly have that running in his veins? I wondered.

I assumed that Alice would continue to defy the goddess and refuse to hand over her child. Yet, if she fought, I feared for her survival. None of us would leave this place alive.

As if realizing this, Alice walked towards Circe, now holding the child out before her. As she passed Tom and Johnson, she hissed, 'Be awake! Be vigilant! On your feet and stand close together!'

The spooks clambered to their feet, and I did as she'd told me and stood next to Tom, who was watching Alice as if in a dream. As Alice offered Tilda to Circe, Tom gave a growl of anger and lifted his staff. It seemed as if he intended to intervene, preventing the goddess from taking his child. But it was already too late. The smiling Circe was holding the baby and peering closely at the blanket which swaddled her.

From that moment time seemed to slow down. Alice was walking back towards us, her arms held out wide as if to embrace the three of us. But it took so long; it was as if she were swimming against a strong current that kept dragging her backwards.

All at once my gaze was drawn back to the goddess, who was no longer smiling. She shrieked in surprise.

Two long, green-taloned hands were reaching out of the baby's blanket towards her. I saw them gouge at her eyes, watched the red blood spurt as they shredded her face. Using its grip on Circe, the creature emerged from the blanket and wrapped itself around her head so that I could no longer see it. It had several legs, each limb ending in a sharp claw. They began to inflict terrible wounds on her neck and shoulders.

As the goddess screamed, the Magi roared and leaped towards us – but Alice was already hugging the three of us, and the throne room whirled around us and vanished. I seemed to be falling, and then we were on our knees on the hill close to where Alice and I had sat by the fire: we were back in the real world.

'Quickly!' Alice shouted. 'We need to leave now! We may be followed . . .'

Within moments we were hurrying back through the trees towards Salford. Johnson was behind me, his right arm held awkwardly, cursing under his breath. I was directly behind Tom and Alice and I heard everything they said.

'Where's our child?' Tom demanded.

'It's a girl, Tom, and she's called Tilda,' Alice retorted.

'Then where is she, Alice? I need to know!'

'She's safe, Tom. She's with Grimalkin.'

'Then contact her now. Get her to bring her back.'

'I can't. It ain't safe, Tom. Circe ain't finished with us,' Alice cried impatiently. 'She's safer there with Grimalkin. A year and a day she'll keep her, and then bring her back. That's what I agreed. You trust Grimalkin, don't you? She supplied the changeling that attacked Circe.'

'Of course I trust her, but does it have to be so long? A year and a day?' Tom shouted. 'I haven't even seen her. I've never even held my own daughter . . .'

'You would have if you'd stayed for the birth!'

'That's not fair, Alice.'

'Ain't it?' she said angrily. 'Well, how do you think I feel? To give her up broke my heart, it did, and it's still wrenching my insides. But it's not safe to keep Tilda with us. At least she'll be safe with Grimalkin; Circe can't reach her there.

And it gives us time to see about sorting Circe out once and for all. There must be a way, and we've got to find it.'

Suddenly Alice glanced back at me, and then they advanced out of earshot and carried on talking. Clearly they were both upset and angry, and at first they walked apart, but gradually they drifted closer to each other until finally Tom seized Alice's hand and pulled her towards him. Moments later they were kissing and hugging before walking on hand in hand.

After a while Alice dropped back to join me. 'Thanks for being brave, Wulf. You did exactly what I asked. I couldn't tell you what I was going to do because Circe might have sensed your fear. She's well able to read thoughts. It took all my strength to keep her out of my own mind.'

'So Grimalkin is keeping Tilda safe?' I asked her.

'Yes, but *we're* not safe any more. That changeling did some damage to Circe, but she'll soon heal, you mark my words, and then she'll try to harm us. She won't be able to leave her underworld, but she can send others after us – her power might even harm us from afar. It could happen now or it could happen months from now – we'll need to be wary. I've got to find a way to deal with her before Grimalkin gives Tilda back to me, ain't I.'

We were now walking along the main street of Salford. We paused at Johnson's house, and Alice cleaned and bandaged his shoulder. He was furious at the damage the

Quisitor's monks had inflicted. There were books from his library scattered all over the floor, and pages had been ripped out.

However, he left everything as it was, hurriedly gathering together a few things, including two or three books, and packing them in his bag before we set off. We all knew it wasn't safe to stay in Salford. Eventually the abbey would find the dead monks, and work out what had happened. Johnson had left no witnesses, but there was a chance the Church wasn't finished with him yet.

Spook Johnson's days hunting witches in Salford were over. I wondered where he'd go now. At one point on the journey, when Tom and Johnson were walking together, I heard animated voices. I wondered if they were discussing his future plans.

Because now we were heading north towards Chipenden.

26

THE CHOICE

That evening we were sitting around the fire eating more delicious rabbits that Alice had caught and cooked. Both she and Tom were still very upset, but they were trying to put on a brave face. They longed with all their hearts to have Tilda with them, but knew that for now it wasn't possible.

'We've been thinking,' Tom said, turning to me. 'As you won't be going back to the abbey, Alice and I would like to offer you a home with us . . .'

From across the fire Alice smiled at me in agreement. I returned her smile. Tom clearly took this to mean I'd accepted, as he continued:

'Well, that's your home sorted out, so now we need to talk about your job. I might be able to find a local farmer who'd take you on, if that's what you want – but when we spoke earlier,' he added, 'Will Johnson confirmed what I'd already suspected for a while – that you're the seventh son of a seventh son . . . which means you could become my apprentice!'

'Now just wait a minute!' Johnson growled from my left. 'You never mentioned making such an offer to the boy. I've already offered him an apprenticeship with me, and he's considering the offer. Isn't that right, boy?'

I looked at Johnson, and nodded in confirmation. It was true, after all. The smile had slipped from Alice's face, and Tom just shrugged.

'When you're fit again, Will, there are two areas in the County that desperately need the services of a spook,' he said to Johnson, smiling pleasantly. 'There's a spook's house up on Anglezarke Moor, and another on the edge of a marsh, near the canal north of Caster. I'm always being summoned to help there – the marsh is plagued with water witches. Both houses were left to me in John Gregory's will, but they are available, rent free, to any spook who is prepared to live and work there.'

'The marsh house sounds like my kind of place,' said Johnson. 'Dealing with witches is what I'm good at.'

Alice looked across the fire at him and she wasn't smiling. 'You must choose what's best for you, Will Johnson. But Wulf must choose too. He must choose between Tom and you, and think very carefully about which spook he wants for his master. Only he can decide.'

Johnson opened his mouth as if to protest, but then thought better of it. He nodded, and stuffed it with some more rabbit instead.

I looked from one to the other. I had no difficulty in making up my mind.

Although a decent man at heart and a good, courageous fighter, Johnson was flawed. In addition to his personal failings, his obsession with witches meant that I wouldn't receive the broader training such an apprenticeship demanded.

On the other hand, Tom was more knowledgeable and by far the better spook. He was also calm and civilized, whereas Spook Johnson was volatile and uncouth. Moreover, the boggart cooked an excellent breakfast, and Alice produced even better suppers. With Tom and Alice, I'd be living in a warm, pleasant home – a far cry from the chill austerity of the abbey.

I just had to be diplomatic and take time while I pretended to make up my mind so that Johnson would think I'd considered his offer carefully. From my point of view, everything was settled.

However, the following night everything changed.

Tom and I were walking through a wood, gathering fuel for our new campfire, when we suddenly heard howls in the distance – threatening, bestial cries that lifted the hairs on the back of my neck. I'd heard the howling of wolves before, but this was something far worse.

Then the howling changed to roars.

'Sounds like trouble,' Tom said seriously. 'Let's get back . . .'

We abandoned our bundles of firewood, and raced back through the trees until we reached our camp. Alice was pacing back and forth, looking anxious. Johnson was staring into the trees, his staff gripped in his hands. With his shoulder bandaged and his arm in a sling, I wondered how effective he'd be at wielding it. Then again, I thought, I had underestimated him before . . .

'Circe has done what I feared. She's sent the Magi after us,' Alice reported. 'Keep going north. I'll sort them out as best I can.'

Tom Ward shook his head. 'No, Alice. I can't have you risking yourself when you've done so much already. I'm the one who should deal with this.'

The howling and roaring started up again; this time it sounded much nearer.

'We're about five miles from the nearest ley line,' Tom said, scratching his head. 'It's too far to get help from Kratch.'

'Kratch? You mean the boggart?' I asked.

He nodded. 'I could summon it down the ley line but we're too far away. We'd never reach it in time.'

'Two spooks should be more than a match for what's out there,' Johnson declared, appearing at Tom Ward's side.

Tom shook his head again. 'You're hurt, Will. Don't worry, I can handle this. I'd be obliged if you'd head north with Alice and Wulf. They'll need you if it comes to a fight later.'

Spook Johnson protested, but when Alice joined her voice to Tom's he seemed to realize he had to go along with it.

I was puzzled when Tom asked me to look after his bag and staff. What would he use to defend himself? I wondered. After giving Alice a long hug and whispering a few words to her, he headed off into the trees towards the threatening howls with nothing to defend himself.

We turned and headed north at a brisk pace.

However, after a while Alice put her hand on my shoulder and stopped, drawing me to one side, out of Spook Johnson's hearing.

'I'd like you to go after Tom,' she said. 'Don't worry, Wulf. I don't want you to actually help him deal with those things. Just keep well back until it's over. I'm sure he's going to be all right, but he may be a little confused when it's over. So please bring him back . . .'

'Confused?' I asked, confused myself.

'Yes, he might not be quite himself. Don't be afraid though. He wouldn't hurt a hair on your head. Just remind him who you are and call out his name. He'll follow you back to me. Could you do that for me, Wulf?'

I nodded. How could I refuse Alice after all she'd done for me?

Still carrying Tom's staff and bag, I suppressed every instinct that told me to flee and set off towards the howling creatures. I was filled with dread: I might find Tom hurt, or even worse. How could he hope to defend himself against those creatures with no weapons to hand? And, if he couldn't deal with them, then I'd be their next victim. I could never refuse Alice – and she never seemed to have any qualms about sending me off into danger.

It was almost dark, and the wood was gloomy and full of shadows. All at once the sounds ahead became even more terrifying – a loud roar punctuated by shrill screams. I hoped that it wasn't Tom screaming in pain.

As I advanced fearfully through the trees, I saw evidence that some sort of violent struggle had taken place. There was a lot of blood splattered across a tree trunk, and what looked like pieces of an animal dotted the grass – bloodied clumps of black-and-white fur attached to flesh and fragments of bone. Was that one of the Magi? I wondered. How could that be possible?

The sudden scream directly ahead of me was so shrill that it hurt my ears, and I almost dropped the staff and bag as

I struggled to cover them with my hands. I stood there trembling, unable to take another step towards that terrible sound.

Then I realized that something large was moving through the trees. I could hear it padding heavily towards me, breaking branches and snapping twigs as it approached. When I saw it, my heart lurched inside my chest and almost stopped beating.

Its cruel eyes were red vertical slits that glowed in the gloom, and its huge body was feline, sleek fur patterned with black-and-white stripes. Those eyes looked into mine, and I knew instantly that I was as good as dead. The mouth opened to reveal the deadly fangs, and the creature roared and bounded towards me.

Terrified, but no longer frozen to the spot, I dropped the bag and held Tom Ward's staff in both hands, fumbling for the catch that would release the silver-alloy blade at its tip. I heard the click as it emerged, and I pointed it at the beast, struggling to hold it steady.

Against that huge predator, I had no chance at all. I remembered how Circe had described its methods of hunting. It could tear out my throat so that I would choke and gasp in agony as my blood gushed forth. Or maybe it would simply crush my skull in its powerful jaws. Or, worst of all, it might play with me, delighting in my torment as it gripped me in its jaws and then used the claws on its hind legs to lacerate my stomach and disembowel me.

The monster's huge eyes were locked on mine as its paws thumped down on the ground. I was numb, the staff shaking in my hands; I was just waiting for death. I muttered a quick prayer to St Andrew Avellino, the patron saint of those fearing a violent death. The saint didn't respond.

But something else did.

There was a blur of motion from my right. Just before the creature reached me, something collided with it and swept it away. I turned to see two beasts locked together in a life-and-death struggle. One was the huge cat pawing the air, its talons frantically seeking flesh while its jaws roared forth its fury. The other, covered in blood and vaguely human in shape, sat on the back of the cat, both arms wrapped around its neck. At first I thought it was trying to strangle it but, as it forced the head further and further back, I guessed that it was trying to break its neck.

There was a loud crack. The roaring ceased and the beast went limp. Trembling with fear, I watched the monster that had slain it clamber to its feet. What on earth was this terrible beast? Would I be its next victim? I thought as I stood there, frozen.

As it fixed its pitiless gaze upon me, the world spun, and I staggered and almost fell. Having neither the will nor the courage to defend myself, I let the staff fall to the ground.

The creature's face resembled that of a human but was covered in green scales and elongated, the long jaw jutting forward. The mouth was wide and the teeth were needle-sharp. The scaled hands were larger than those of a man, and each finger ended in a long sharp talon. It had clothes that were saturated in red blood, and black boots; the right one, I saw, was tied not with a lace but with string.

Then the truth finally pierced my befuddled brain. I knew this monster.

It was Tom Ward.

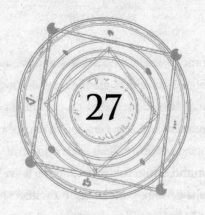

THE FACE OF CIRCE

As the Spook started to walk towards me, there was no recognition in his eyes. His gaze was pitiless. He'd changed into something that was so far from being human that he might kill me without a thought.

Then I remembered what Alice had told me . . .

Just remind him who you are and call his name. He'll follow you back to me.

I felt far from certain that this would work, but I called out anyway.

'Tom! Tom!' I shouted. 'It's me, Wulf!'

There was still no recognition in his eyes, though he halted five paces short of me.

'Follow me, Tom. I'll lead you back to Alice,' I went on firmly.

He didn't move, just stared at me and gave a deep growl. I wondered if he was angry; maybe he was about to leap on me and snap my neck? I realized that he must be incredibly strong to have broken the neck of that cat-beast. Then I remembered the pieces of flesh on the ground – flesh with tufts of black-and-white fur. It must have been the remains of another of the Magi – did he rip it to pieces? And where was the third? Had he killed that too?

I had to try to get him back to Alice as quickly as possible. I certainly didn't want to be alone with him any longer than I had to.

'Follow me, Tom!' I called again. Then I picked up the bag and staff, carefully turned my back on him and began to walk away.

I was holding my breath, fearing a sudden onslaught from behind, but then I heard him coming and gave a sigh of relief.

The moon rose into the sky, painting everything with its silver light. For hours we walked north towards Chipenden, following the path Alice and Spook Johnson had taken. The thing that was Tom Ward was behind me all the time. I did not expect to catch the others soon. They would be walking quickly; our pace was quite slow.

I was suddenly aware that I could no longer hear the footsteps behind me, and I turned to see Tom veering away towards a clump of bushes and trees. I followed him, keeping some distance between us. He knelt down on the bank of a small stream. I heard him sip from the water, then he began to sluice his face, hands and arms, washing away the blood.

When he turned his face up to the moonlight, I saw that the scales were gone. He was himself again. He gave me a weary smile. 'Thanks for coming after me and leading me in the right direction, Wulf,' he said gratefully.

'You should thank Alice,' I told him. 'It was her idea.'

He nodded, and drank from the stream again. Then he held out his hand for the staff and I handed it to him, though I kept the bag, carrying it for him as if I were his apprentice. We set off again, walking side by side now.

I glanced down at his hands and saw that they too had returned to normal. All that was left of that human-shaped monster was the blood that it had spilled. It still soaked his garments and its coppery stink was very strong upon the air.

'I wish you hadn't seen that, Wulf,' Tom said at last. 'I think I owe you an explanation.'

I didn't reply. I was still in a state of shock.

He went on: 'Like you, Wulf, I'm the seventh son of a seventh son, and that gives us both abilities that help us to fight the dark . . .'

Something awful occurred to me. 'Could I change in the same way?' I asked, terrified. What must it be like to transform into such a terrible beast, your mind no longer your own? You might kill a friend or a member of your own family; kill without knowing what you did.

Tom shook his head and reached across to pat me on the shoulder. I couldn't help myself – I flinched, and he withdrew his hand. I saw the disappointment on his face.

'No, Wulf, you wouldn't change like I did. You see, I've something in addition to what we share – it's what I inherited from my mam. She was a lamia . . .'

I remembered what Circe had said about Tom's lamia blood. I also remembered reading something about lamias in Spook Johnson's library.

'That's a type of witch,' I said. 'They can shift their shape from human to . . .'

I left the rest of the sentence unsaid.

Tom nodded. 'Lamia witches are slow shape-shifters who take two main forms. The first is called a domestic lamia, and it's indistinguishable from a human except for one thing. They have a line of green and yellow scales along their spine. But they can slowly change into what's known as a feral lamia. These creatures scuttle around on four legs; they are covered in scales and have a mouthful of fangs that can crunch bones and tear flesh.

'My mother was domestic, as well as being benign. She was the best mother anyone could hope to have. She loved my dad, and helped work the farm and bring up seven sons. Nevertheless her lamia blood runs in my veins as surely as does that of my father. When I'm in extreme danger, I change into a form that can better defend itself.'

'Can you control the change?' I asked.

'I'm slowly getting better at it – but, no, I can't fully control it. That's why I left my staff and bag behind; when I faced those creatures I wanted to be totally unarmed. My life was in extreme peril and an attack would trigger the change. And, of course, when it's all over it takes a while before I'm aware of who I am and what's happened. That's why Alice sent you after me.'

I nodded and we continued on in silence. I was thinking over what he'd said; I was far from happy. I'd judged Tom to be calm and civilized – a man who would make a good master, a teacher and colleague. But he too was flawed. Dark blood ran in his veins. It was that blood and the fact that he was the seventh son of a seventh son that had driven Circe to seek out his child: a child that also had Alice's blood.

Alice had been good to me, but there was no denying that she was a powerful witch. No wonder they had formed such a close bond and had a child together.

I reflected that, despite his best intentions, Tom might change from man to beast at any time. Those big cats had scared me, but after he had slain them and turned his gaze upon me, I had known terror such as I had never experienced before.

I certainly had a difficult decision to make, though I felt uncomfortable walking alongside Tom Ward now. I couldn't get what I'd seen out of my head. Fortunately, Alice and Johnson were waiting for us not too far ahead. I was glad of their company.

In the late evening of the following day we finally reached the house close to Chipenden. We were all weary and footsore, and went to bed as soon as we arrived, too tired even to bother with supper.

Once again Tom directed me to the room with the green door: the one that had been used by so many spook's apprentices over the years. Before climbing into bed, I looked once more at the names scratched onto the wall. There was possibly just enough room to add my own, but it would have to be written in extremely small script.

But I knew I would never write my name there. After what I'd seen, I was going to be Spook Johnson's apprentice, not Tom Ward's.

I blew out the candle and climbed between the cool sheets, feeling better now that I'd made my decision.

However, almost immediately I sensed a sinister coldness in the air. No, not now, I thought . . . Hadn't I faced enough? After all that, the demon was here to torment me again. I was terrified. It seemed that even in the house of the Spook, the demon could still reach me.

I gazed up, and saw the shadow of the stick-demon beginning to form on the ceiling.

I cringed, expecting taunts or sudden agonizing pain, but instead I was stunned by what confronted me.

This time the demon had a face.

It was the face of Circe.

'*Now you know who I truly am, priest,*' taunted the goddess. '*I have enjoyed tormenting you and bending you to my will. I sent you north to Chipenden to lure Tom Ward into my clutches. I knew that once I had her beloved spook, Alice Deane would hasten to his aid, bringing her child with her.*'

'You planned all that from the start?' I asked, slowly realizing the extent of Circe's deception.

'*Yes! You were my little puppet, so easy to direct. Afterwards I would have let you go free, allowed you to resume your little life. But you betrayed me. You made it possible for Alice to deceive me and escape. For that there is no forgiveness! Very soon I will slay the two spooks and Alice Deane. Then I will slay you. The child will be mine sooner or later, its blood mine to sip. And all will have been for nothing. So here is something as a foretaste of that . . .*'

Then the pain began, and it was worse than it had ever been.

I convulsed and arched my back, fearing as I always did that my spine would snap. This time it really felt like it would.

I began to scream in agony.

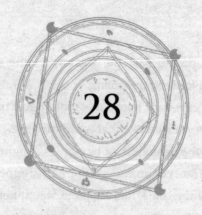

28

THE WANDERING SPOOK

My screams brought Alice running to the bedroom.

'Wulf? Are you all right?' she called, knocking on my door. 'What's happening!'

'Help!' I cried, and she wrenched open the door and strode in carrying a candle. Her eyes widened as she saw my body arched and twisted under the blanket. Then her expression darkened in anger as she saw the image on the ceiling directly above the bed.

'Avaunt! Be gone!' Alice cried.

For a moment nothing happened; then the face of Circe twisted in scorn and there was a roar like that of some wild beast. A powerful wind buffeted the room, lifting the curtains, blowing out Alice's candle and sending her crashing back against the door.

The room was dark, but the glowing figure of a triumphant Circe was still visible on the ceiling. My pain had eased a little, I thought as I sat up, but now I prepared myself for the agony to be intensified – for how could Alice win?

Suddenly a bright light flared like sheet lightning – but it came from Alice, not from Circe. She had dropped the candle and was holding both hands outstretched, her forefingers pointing directly at the image on the ceiling. Another kind of lightning, blue and forked, exploded from her fingers to obliterate the image of Circe.

Again the room grew dark . . . but then Alice was holding the candle again, its flame shining brightly. Even as she held it aloft, the candle I'd placed on the window ledge also flickered into life. I realize that both had been lit by Alice's magic: the same magic that had driven Circe away.

There was a smell of burning, and Alice pointed up at the ceiling, where the plaster was singed and smoking.

'Tom ain't going to be pleased at that!' she said with a smile.

As she drew closer to the bed, I held the blanket up to my chin. I was still trembling with pain. It felt as if flames were burning inside me while needles pierced my limbs.

She pulled up the small chair and sat close to me. I was still whimpering and groaning with pain, but when Alice placed her hand on my brow it ceased immediately.

Still, it was a long time before my breathing and heart rate slowed and I was able to speak. Finally I told her what had happened and how Circe had manipulated me.

'I'm sorry, Alice,' I said in conclusion. 'A lot of what's happened was my fault.'

She shook her head. 'You're always blaming yourself, Wulf. That ain't necessary. The only thing you did wrong was not telling me about your visitations when we first met. I could have done something about them – though that wouldn't have changed nothing. Tom's sense of duty would always have sent him off to Salford to help Johnson. That's just the way he is. And because I'm the way I am, I'd always have followed him there with Tilda. Don't you worry. Tomorrow I'll give you something to keep Circe away. So . . . have you finally decided to be apprenticed to Will Johnson?'

Here she was, reading my mind again! I sighed. 'Yes. I'm sorry for not choosing Tom.'

She smiled. 'Don't be. You might change your mind later. Everyone's allowed to do that.'

Spook Johnson and I stayed at the Chipenden house while we regained our strength and his shoulder began to heal. As she had promised, Alice gave me a ward against Circe. It was a little red feather plucked from a robin's breast. While it was in my possession, it would prevent Circe's spirit intruding into my mind.

I was sad when the time came to leave the warmth and security of that home – it was a safe place to be – but at last, after breakfast on the third morning after our arrival, we took our leave. We were heading for the house north of Caster that stood near the canal.

Johnson didn't waste time on goodbyes, and set off at a fast pace, swaggering as usual. I gave Tom a final wave, then turned and hurried at my master's heels, carrying his bag. I had told Tom my decision face to face, but I hadn't explained how I'd arrived at it. We hadn't mentioned the night he'd changed into a lamia.

We'd only just left the garden when we saw Alice approaching us through the trees. I hadn't heard a sound and she startled me. Sometimes she almost seemed to float rather than walk.

'My good wishes to you, Will Johnson. May you prosper and be safe. I just want a last word with Wulf,' she told him.

He gave the faintest of smiles and nodded in acknowledgement. Then he turned to me. 'Don't dawdle too long, boy. You'll catch me up in five minutes if you know what's good for you.'

Alice moved close and gave me a warm smile. 'You've made a mistake, Wulf. You'd have been better off with Tom,' she said quietly. 'I won't ask you for your reasoning but I have my suspicions.'

I didn't reply. I couldn't meet her gaze, so I looked down at my boots.

'Well, we'll all just have to make the best of it. Ain't a total disaster after all. Just keep your wits about you and you'll be fine. And if you ever do change your mind, Tom will still be happy to take you on as his apprentice.

'I've something more to say to you, Wulf. There are two things you got to watch out for. The first is Circe. You've got the feather to keep her spirit away, and I don't reckon she can actually leave her underworld. But she might send something else – something worse than those great big cats.'

'Worse than them?' I asked fearfully.

'No point in trying to hide the truth from you, Wulf. You need to be vigilant and prepare for anything. You got to watch out for the Bishop of Blackburn too. There might soon be more of them quisitors searching for you and Johnson . . .'

'That's right – the Bishop appointed three of them,' I remembered. Most likely the Church wasn't done with me either.

'There you are then. The remaining two might come after you. So take care. Here's something that might help . . .'

I wondered what it was. I already had the feather.

Alice held out a small, thin, oblong object. She turned it over and I saw that it was a mirror. 'Having begun training as a monk, you're still scared of magic no doubt. But it has already saved your life more than once. So, take this . . .'

I accepted it – though it just looked like an ordinary mirror to me. 'Is there some sort of spell on it?' I asked.

Alice shook her head. 'The magic is in me, ain't it, not the mirror. Any mirror will do for what I have in mind, but this will fit in your pocket. If you're in danger, just breathe on the glass and think of me, or call my name. Then I'll be in touch, and Tom or I will try to help you. Promise you'll do that, Wulf.'

'Yes, I promise. Thanks, Alice,' I said, gazing into the trees, my eyes following the path that Johnson had taken. He'd already be getting impatient.

'Don't worry about that Johnson – he'll just have to wait. Do him good to learn a bit of patience,' Alice said. 'But I want to tell you one more thing, and this is about you and what you are . . .'

'You mean me being the seventh son of a seventh son?' I asked.

'That's it, Wulf, because I don't think you are one.'

'But the Abbot *told* Spook Johnson that I was the seventh son of a seventh son,' I protested.

'The Abbot could have lied, Wulf. He wanted to get you into Johnson's house so that you could spy on him. The Bishop was breathing down his neck to get evidence against spooks. Were you the seventh son in your own family?'

'I was the fourth and last son, but I know that my mother had already lost some children in childbirth or soon after they were born. She never talked about them though. And I'm not sure how many there were or whether they were boys or girls.'

Alice nodded. 'Look, you got all the things you need to become a spook. Tom's been telling me about you, he has. I know you see the dead, and that's one ability given to seventh sons of seventh sons. But there's something else: you pray to the saints, and they sometimes respond, don't they? You saw the arm of a saint reach across and unlock the door of the farmhouse – the one where the child was trapped by a boggart?'

'Yes,' I replied, unsure what she meant. Surely Alice didn't believe in saints?

'Well, seventh sons of seventh sons can't do that. You're something new, Wulf. I don't know what, but I'll find out. It's good to know who we are. It stops us losing ourselves . . .'

Her last remark was mysterious, and I was going to ask her about it, but then she smiled again and sent me on my way. 'Off you go and catch up with Johnson before he starts complaining. And one last thing – don't let him bully you!'

'I won't!' I promised, then set off after my new master. After a couple of steps I turned to give Alice a wave, but she'd already disappeared.

The moment we entered the old millhouse, Johnson told me to get on with the chores. It was a cold, bleak and damp place – a far cry from the house at Chipenden. There was a canal nearby and, to the west, a marsh shrouded in mist. That was where the water witches were supposedly most numerous.

I'd only just managed to get the fires burning in the kitchen grate and under the oven when he set me a more important task – to fill his big belly.

'I'm famished, boy! Make up the other fires later. Fry me my usual five big pork sausages – hot and greasy, just as I like 'em!'

We'd brought some provisions with us, including six bottles of red wine, but to my disappointment there were only six sausages wrapped up in the piece of paper. That meant just one for me.

However, I went into the kitchen and fried all six, buttering lots of thick slices of bread – I'd have to fill my own hungry belly somehow. Soon we were sitting down at the table.

Johnson had drunk the first bottle of wine while I was cooking. Nothing had changed regarding his table manners: as usual he shovelled bread and sausages into his open mouth as quickly as he could. His arm was still in a sling, but he was somehow managing to fork it all in with his left hand.

All at once, in the far distance, we heard a shriek. It came from the direction of the marsh.

'That was a water witch,' the Spook said with a grin. 'That sound is music to my ears! Do you know,' he went on, 'I think I'm going to enjoy it here. A man needs to keep busy, and there'll be lots of water witches to kill. Still, we won't get too comfortable. I stayed too long in Salford and now I'm thinking of travelling a bit. Why should a spook stay in one place? I intend to be a peripatetic spook! Know what that means, boy?'

'Yes,' I replied. 'It's from the Latin word *peripateticus*, which means "habitually walking about" – "wandering".'

'That's right, boy. I'm going to wander the County and deal with witches wherever I can find 'em. Being a witch specialist, my services will be in great demand, don't you agree?'

I nodded, eating a thick slice of buttered bread and saving my only sausage for last.

'Yes,' continued Johnson. 'After we've tidied up this place, we'll head straight for Pendle and sort out the witch problem there.'

I'd hardly been listening to him, but as his words slowly sank in, I began to be alarmed.

'I'll kill the Malkin witch assassin first,' he said. 'That should stir things up a bit and flush out our quarry.'

'There are a lot of Pendle witches,' I told him, remembering what Tom had said to me. 'Three main clans, and other smaller ones too. And each one has a witch assassin. It's said that although they quarrel a lot and fight among themselves, they're more than capable of uniting in the face of a common foe. Don't you think that might be a bit more than we can handle?'

He snorted at me in derision. 'Against a veteran witch hunter like me they'll have as much chance as these sausages!' he said, stuffing another into his mouth. He swallowed and then belched very loudly. 'And don't forget I want you to keep writing that book about me. I'll train you better than any spook's apprentice has been trained before, but in return you write that book – it'll be one of your duties. I aim to be a legend in my own lifetime. It's no more than I deserve!'

Suddenly he stared down at my plate. 'Not feeling well, boy? Lost your appetite?' he roared at me across the table, spitting specks of food into my face. 'Just having a single measly sausage?'

'There were only six sausages,' I told him, slightly annoyed.

He looked at both plates, and then he astonished me again. 'I'm good to my apprentices. I expect them to work hard and obey orders, but never let it be said that I allow them to starve!' he declared.

I couldn't believe it. Using his fork, he transferred the final sausage from his own plate to mine.

It was more amazing than watching him dance.

JOSEPH DELANEY used to be an English teacher, before becoming the best-selling author of the Spook's series, which has been translated into thirty languages and sold millions of copies. The first book, *The Spook's Apprentice*, was made into a major motion picture starring Jeff Bridges and Julianne Moore.

IF YOU'D LIKE TO LEARN MORE ABOUT JOSEPH AND HIS BOOKS, VISIT:

www.josephdelaneyauthor.com

www.penguin.co.uk

THE SPOOK'S SERIES

JOSEPH DELANEY
THE
SPOOK'S
BLOOD

Stand against the dark – or lose everything . . .

JOSEPH DELANEY
THE
SPOOK'S
SLITHER'S TALE

A new darkness is rising . . .

JOSEPH DELANEY
THE
SPOOK'S
ALICE

Will old enemies take their deadly revenge?

JOSEPH DELANEY
THE
SPOOK'S
REVENGE

Everything ends

JOSEPH DELANEY
THE
SPOOK'S
STORIES
WITCHES

Evil has many faces

THE
SPOOK'S
BESTIARY
AS TOLD TO
JOSEPH DELANEY

JOSEPH DELANEY
SPOOK'S
A NEW DARKNESS
THE TIME HAS COME TO FIGHT ALONE

JOSEPH DELANEY
SPOOK'S
THE DARK ARMY

JOSEPH DELANEY
SPOOK'S
DARK ASSASSIN